READY? OK. DRAW A DOT.

NOW DRAW A SMALL DOT.

THEN DRAW A BiG DOT.

DRAW A DOT ON THESE THREE DOTS.

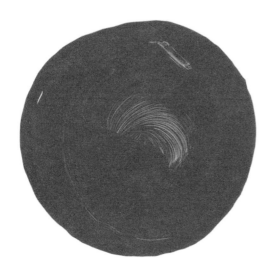 

DRAW LiTTLE DOTS ON THESE LiTTLE DOTS.

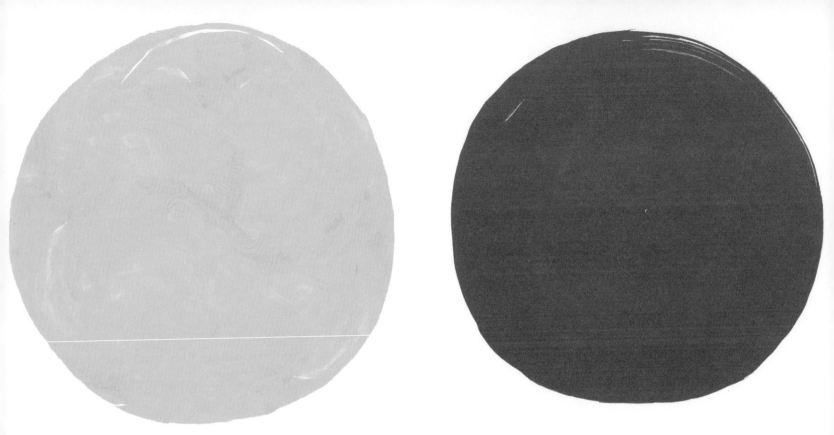

DRAW BIG DOTS ON THESE BIG DOTS.

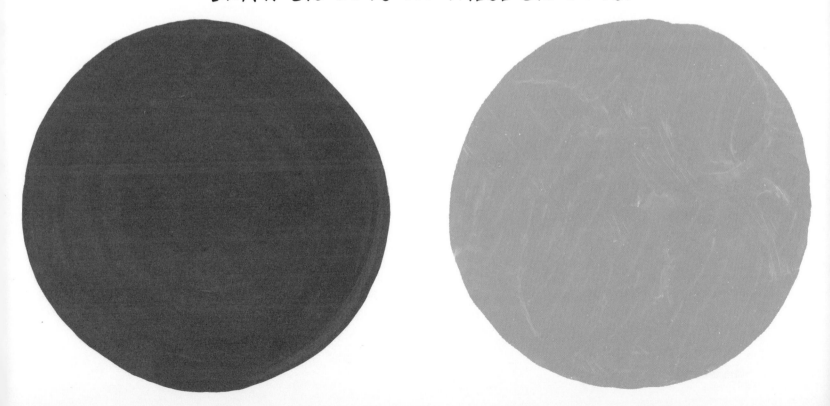

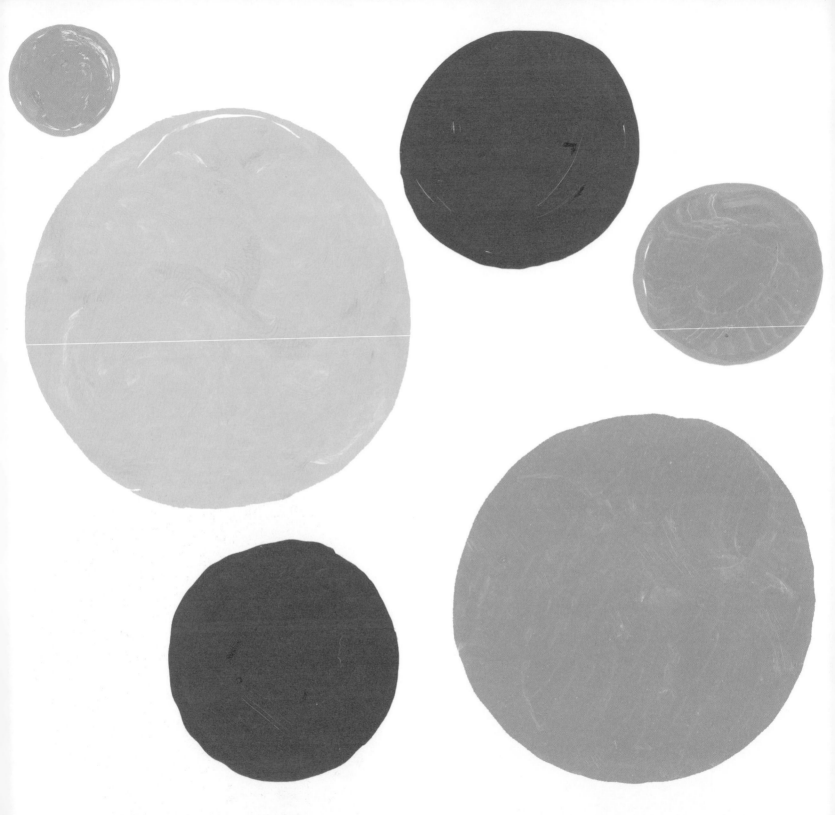

DRAW AS MANY DOTS AS YOU CAN ON THESE DOTS!

FINISH THE PILE OF BIG DOTS.

FINISH THE PILE OF LITTLE DOTS.

DRAW A HUGE PILE OF DOTS!

DRAW DOTS AROUND THESE DOTS.

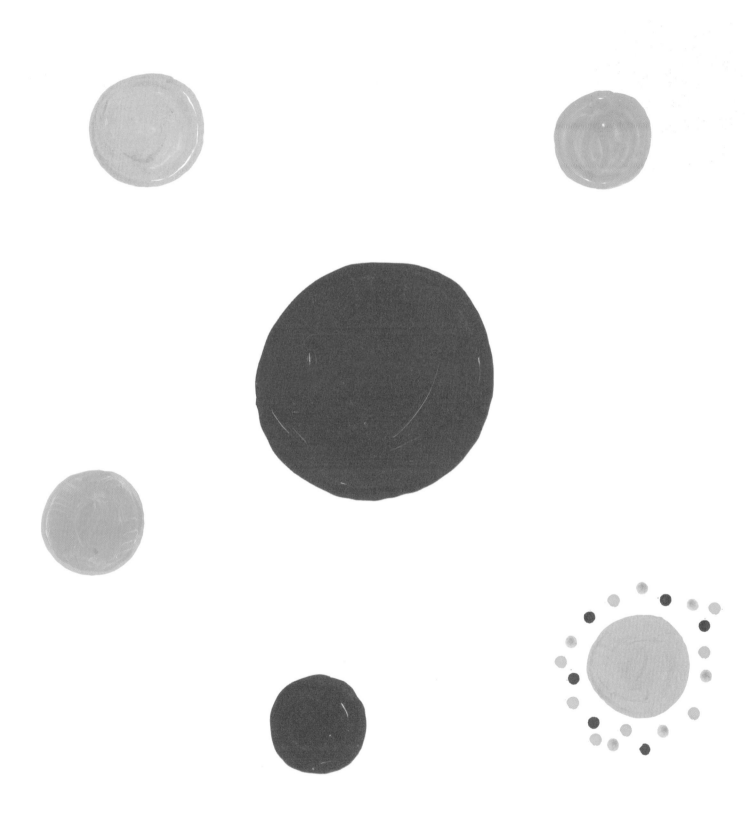

FILL IN THE HOLES IN THESE DOTS.

Fix these dots. Thank you!

DECORATE THESE DOTS . . . USING OTHER DOTS.

KEEP GOING!

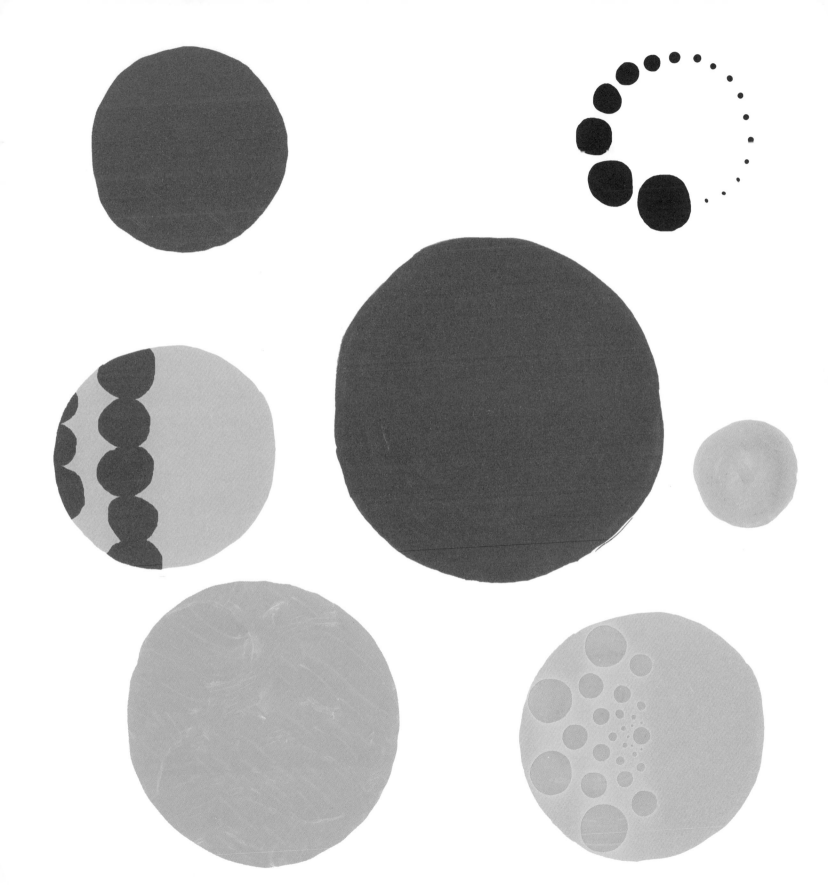

DECORATE THESE DOTS WITH SOME LINES.

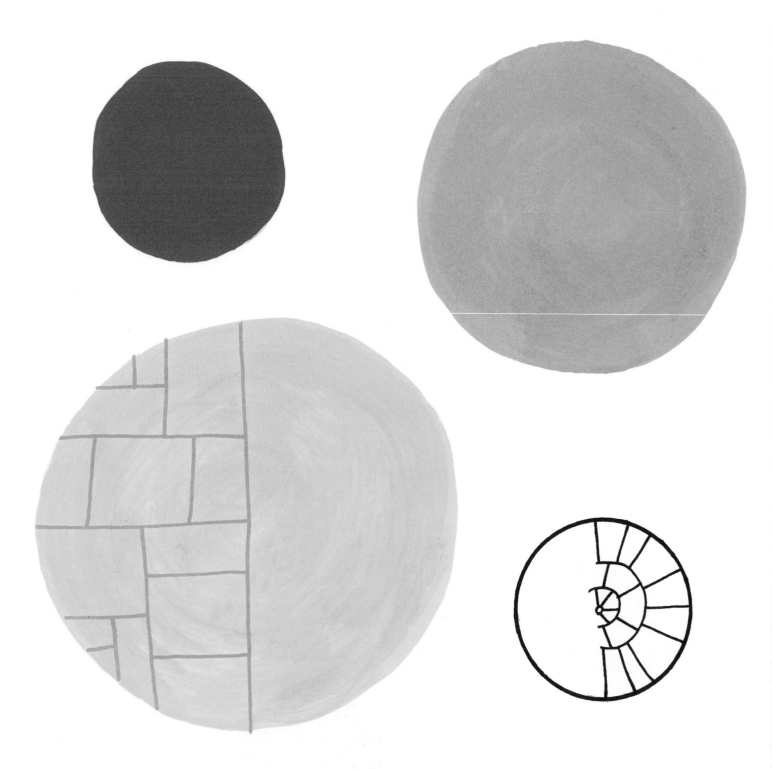

KEEP GOiNG . . . AREN'T THEY PRETTY?

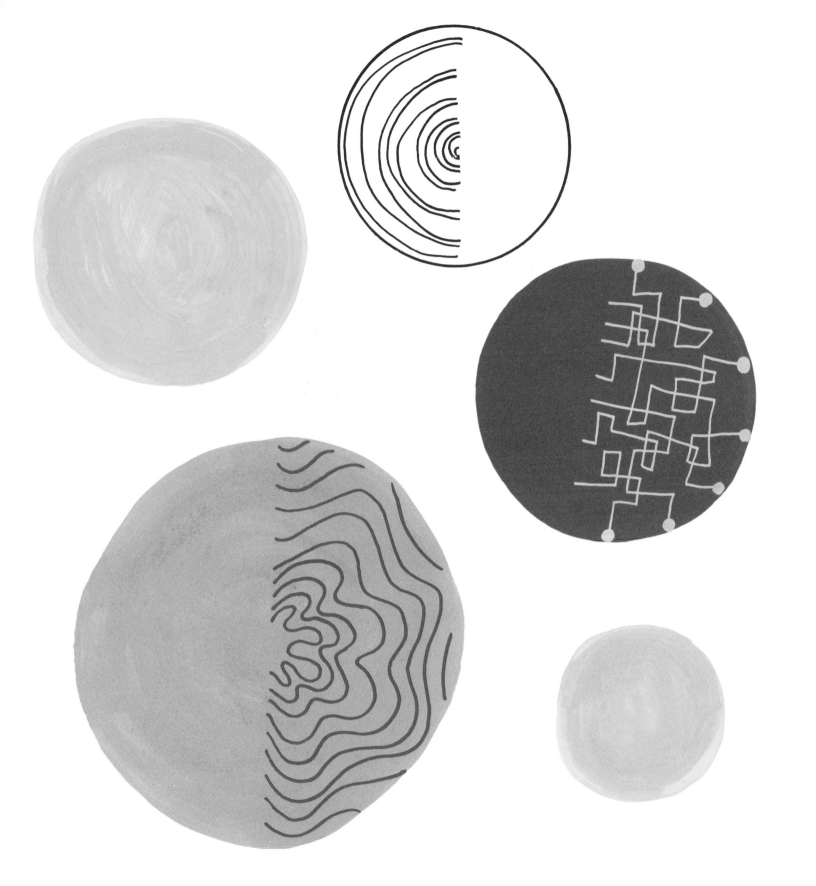

YES! MORE LINES! KEEP GOING . . .

MAKE UP SOME FUN SHAPES TO DRAW
INSIDE EACH DOT.

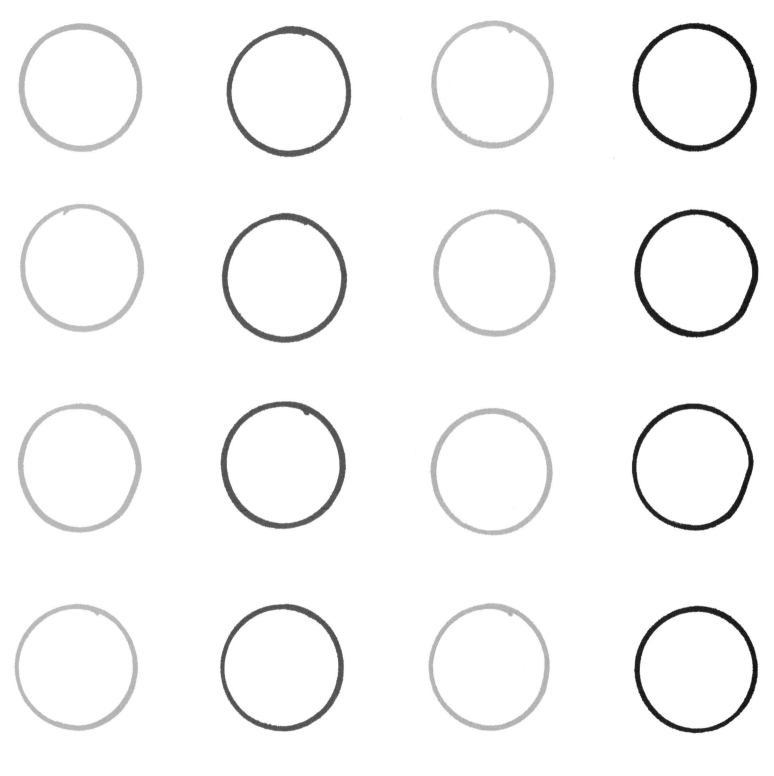

MAKE THESE DOTS THE SAME.

 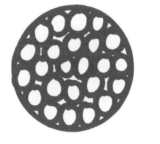  

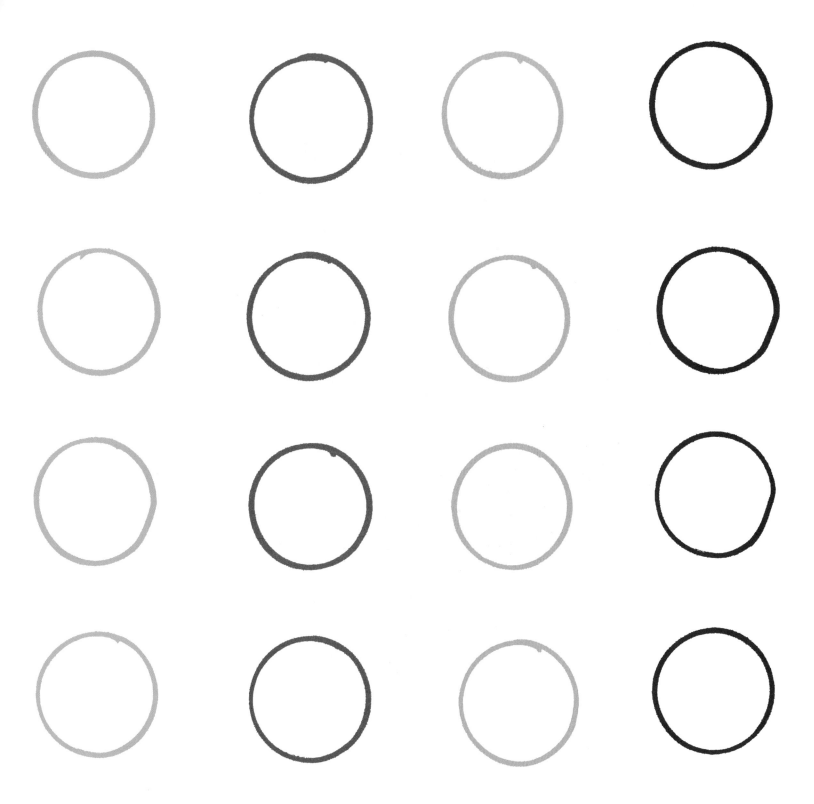

NOW MAKE THEM AS DIFFERENT AS CAN BE!

SCRIBBLE INSIDE THESE DOTS . . . CAREFUL . . .

MAKE SURE TO STAY INSIDE THE CIRCLE!

AGAIN!

SCRIBBLE ON
ONLY THE RED DOTS.

NOW SCRIBBLE ON ALL THE DOTS!

SCRIBBLE AROUND THE DOTS
BUT MAKE SURE NOT TO TOUCH THEM!

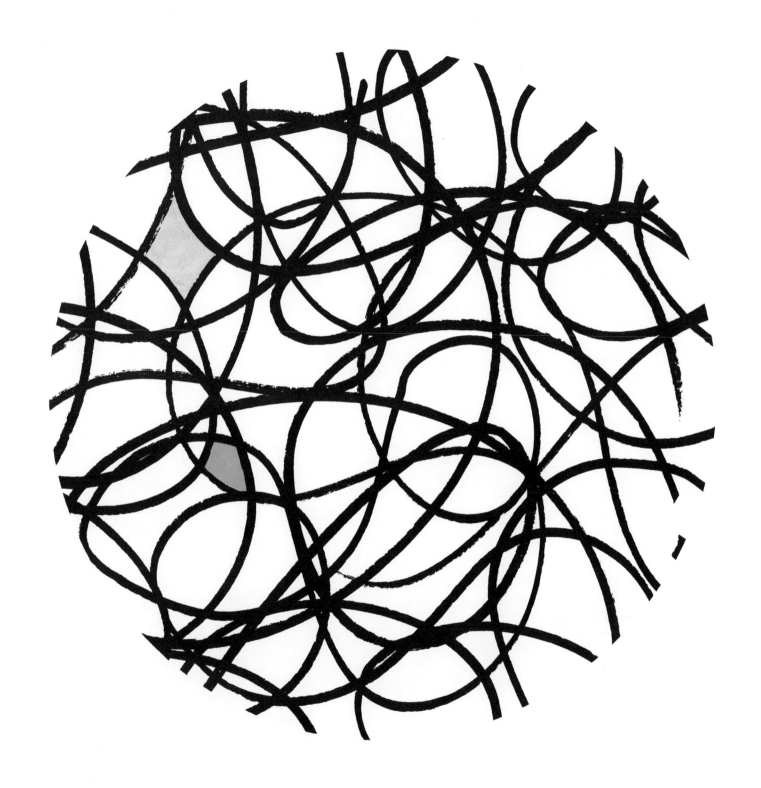

PICK SOME SHAPES TO COLOR IN . . .

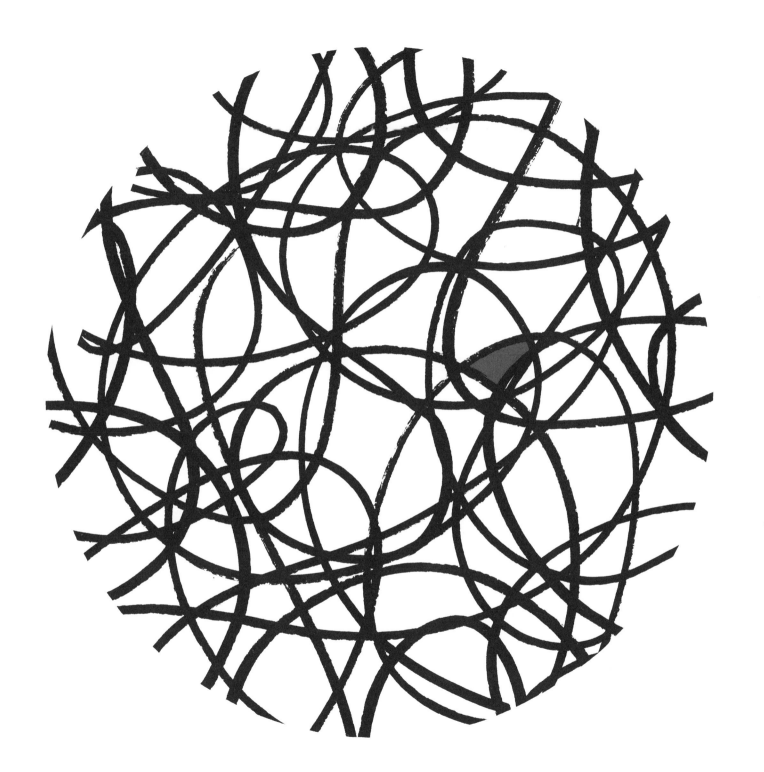

KEEP GOING!

DRAW A DOT IN EVERY LOOP . . .

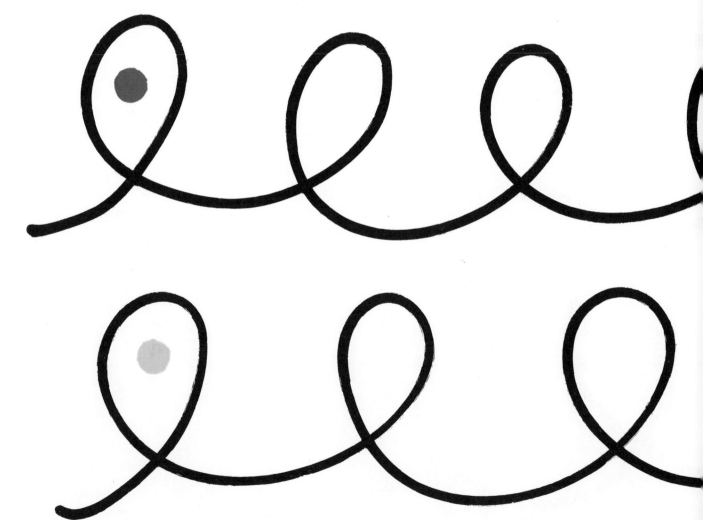

... AND NOW IN EACH OF THESE LOOPS.

OK. NOW DRAW LOOPS AROUND THESE DOTS.

MORE LOOPS . . .

BUT BE CAREFUL NOT TO TOUCH ANY DOTS.

EVEN MORE LOOPS . . .

KEEP GOING . . . FASTER . . . EVEN FASTER!

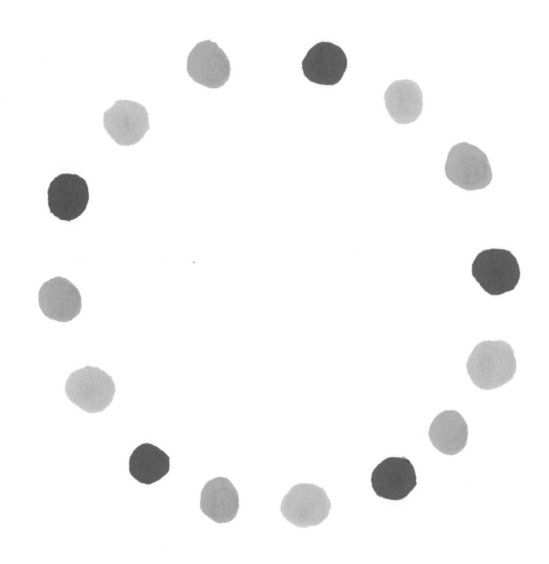

DRAW LOOPS AROUND THESE DOTS.

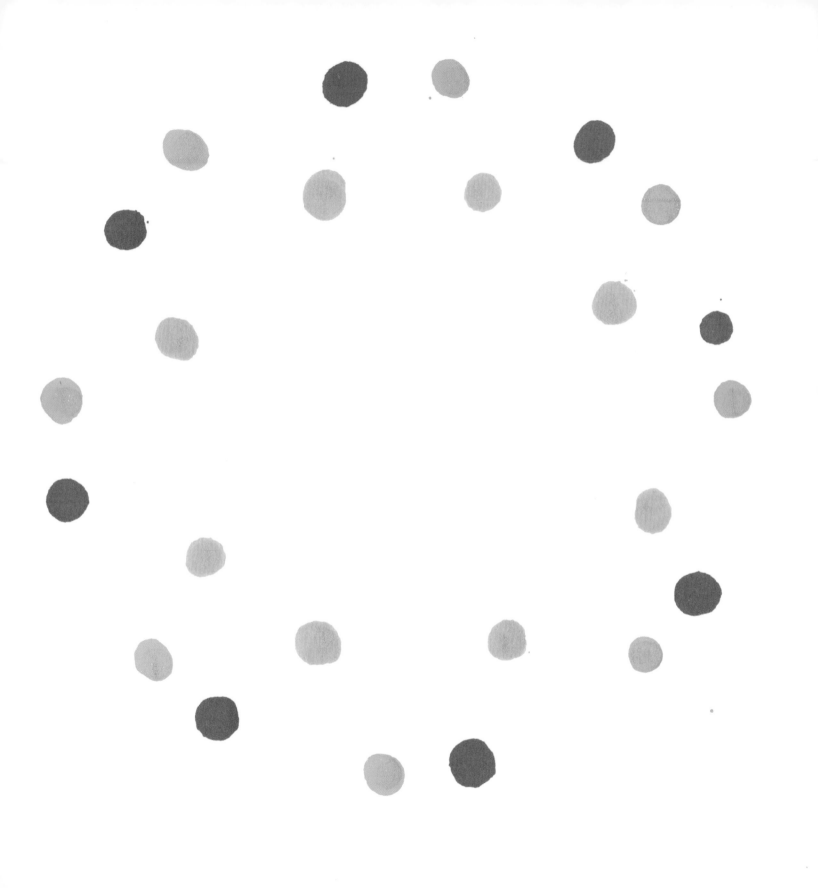

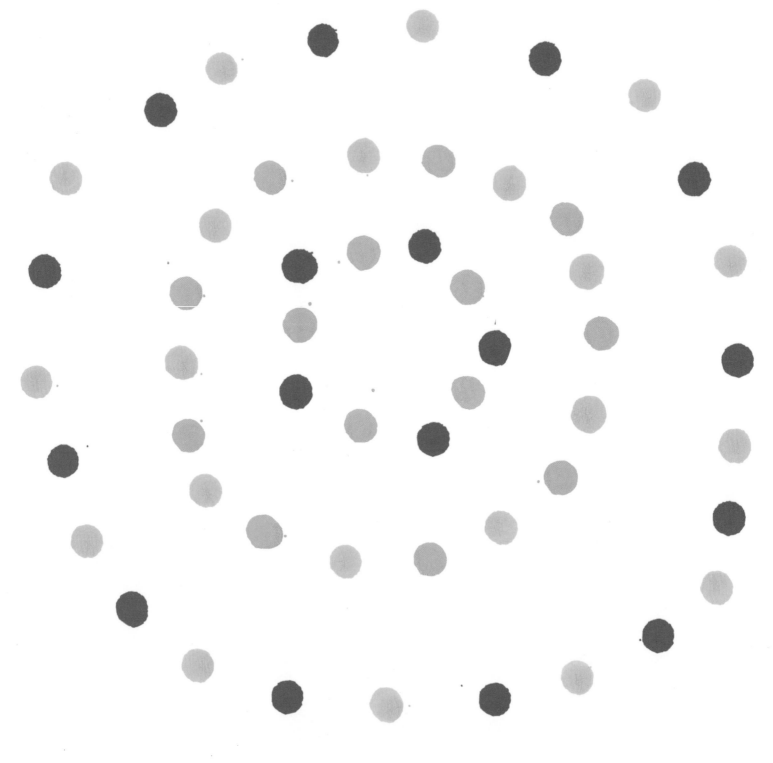

DRAW LOOPS . . .

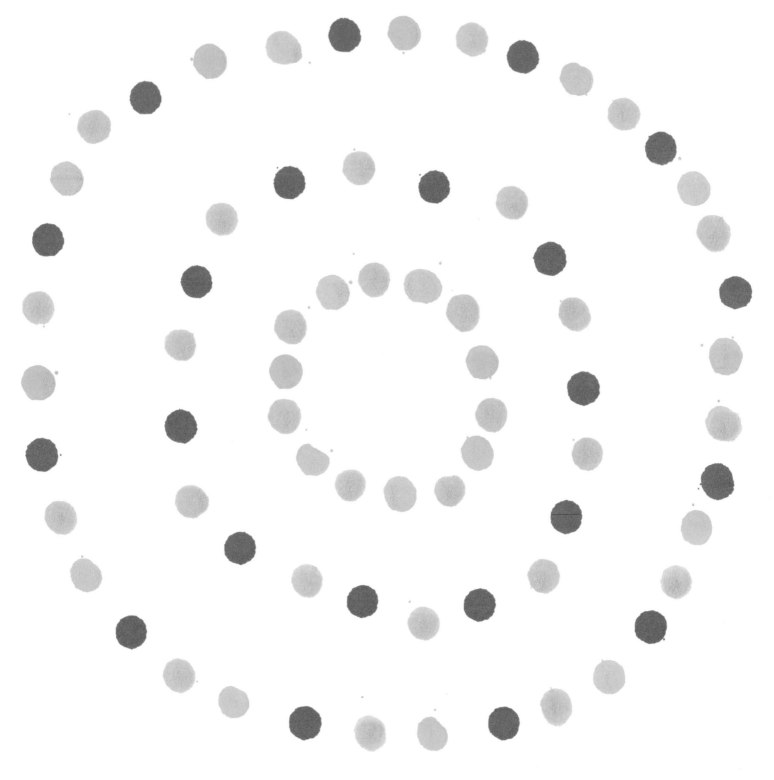

BUT ONLY AROUND THE YELLOW DOTS.

NOW DRAW LOOPS

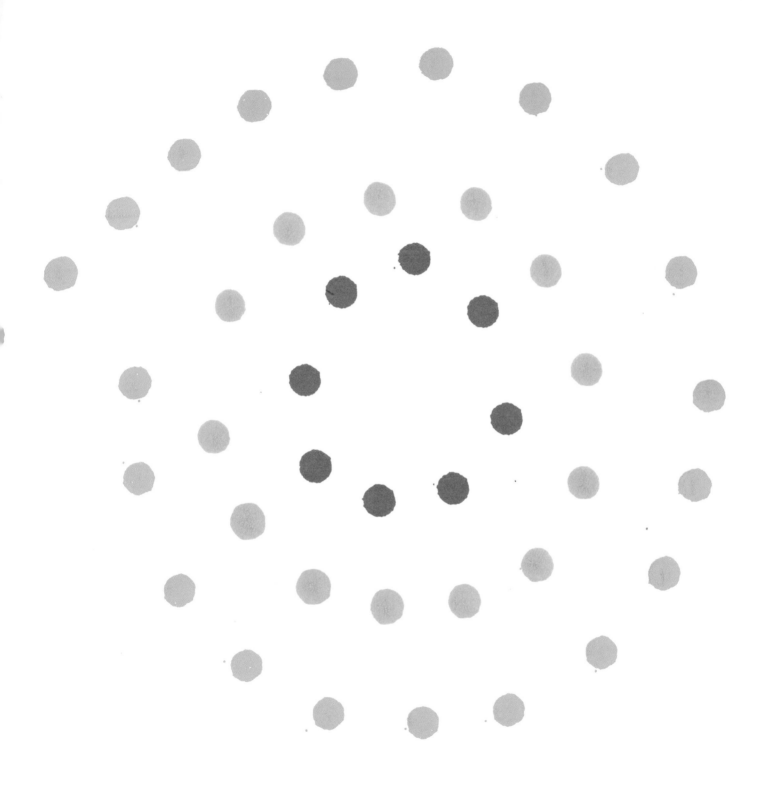

ONLY AROUND THE BLUE DOTS.

AND FINALLY DRAW LOOPS

ONLY AROUND THE RED DOTS.

TURN ↑ THE PAGE QUICKLY AROUND THIS DOT.

NOW ↑ TURN) iT iN THE OPPOSITE DiRECTION.

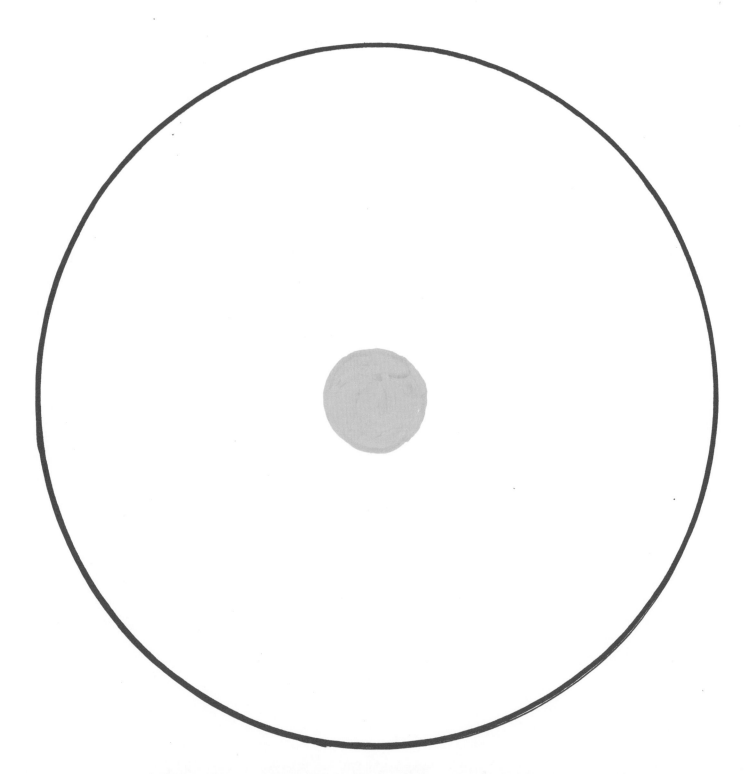

DRAW CiRCLES AROUND THE DOT . . .

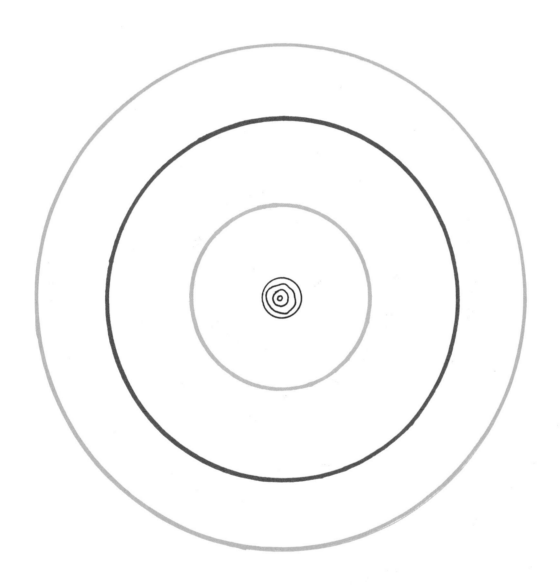

AND DRAW CiRCLES AROUND THOSE CiRCLES.

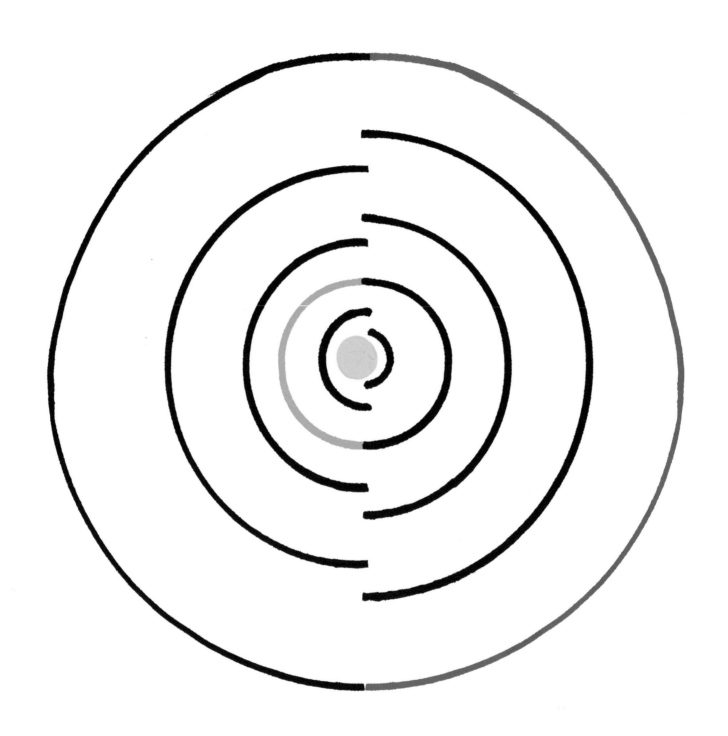

COMPLETE THE CIRCLES.

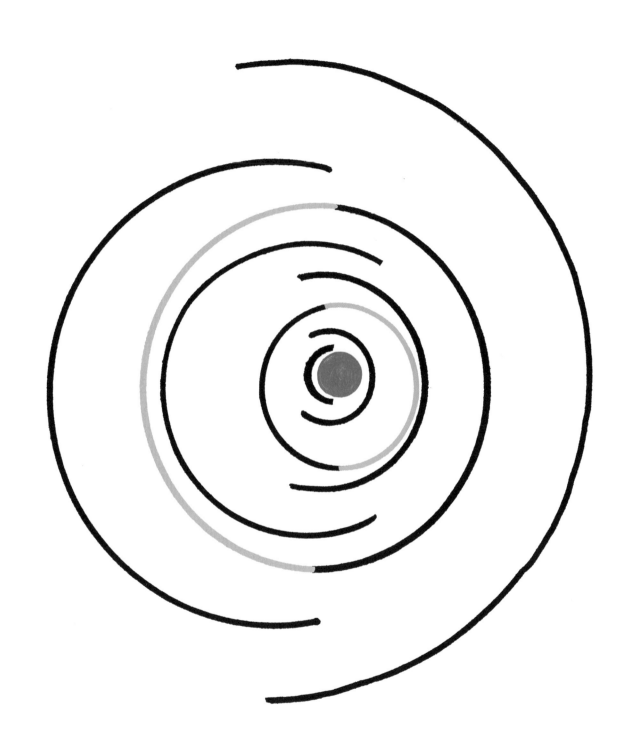

DRAW LOOPS AROUND THE BLUE DOTS . . .

SCRIBBLE ON THE YELLOW DOTS . . .

AND PUT LITTLE DOTS AROUND THE RED DOTS.

DRAW ONE CONTINUOUS LINE . . .   LOOP AROUND
THE BLUE DOTS . . .

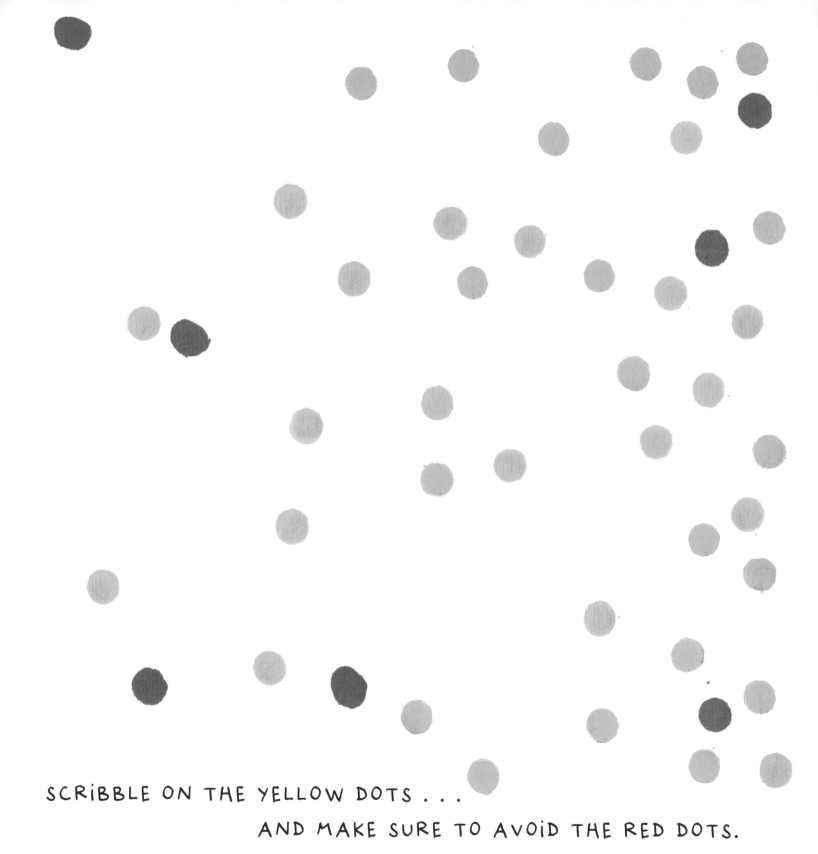

SCRIBBLE ON THE YELLOW DOTS . . .

AND MAKE SURE TO AVOID THE RED DOTS.

CONNECT TWO DOTS OF THE SAME COLOR WITH A LINE.

CONNECT TWO DOTS OF THE SAME COLOR WITH LOOPS.

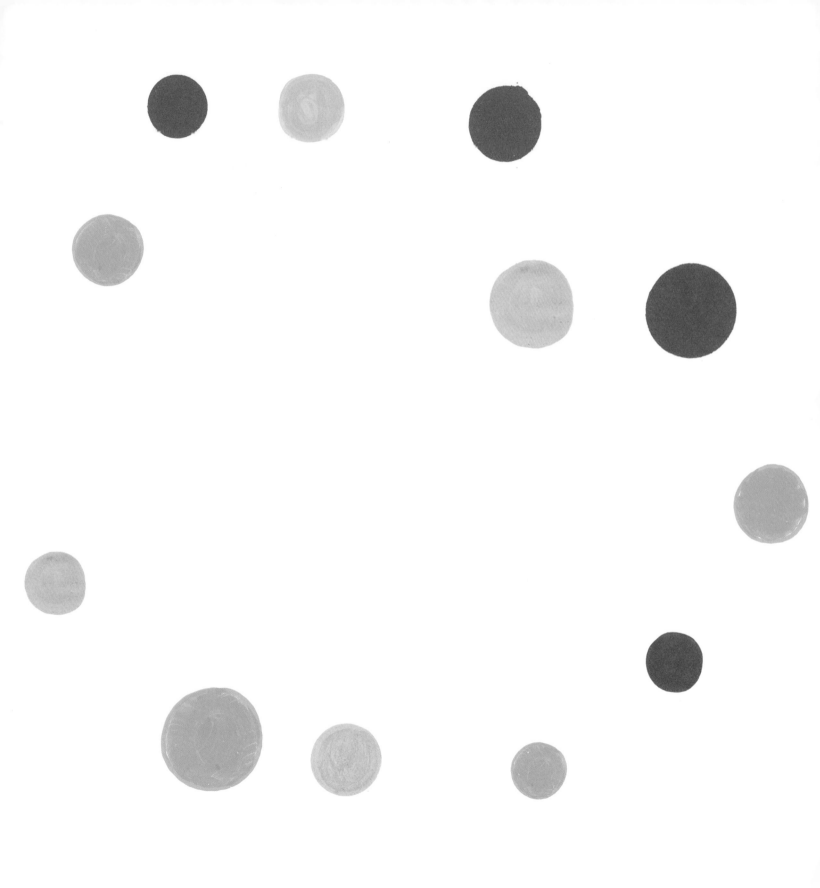

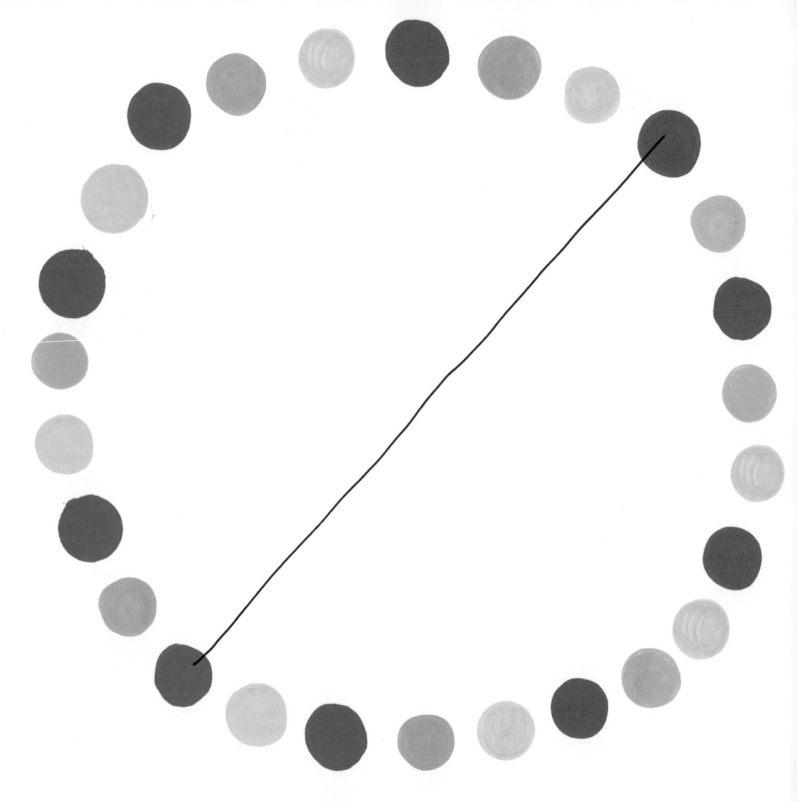

CONNECT TWO DOTS OF THE SAME COLOR WITH A LINE.

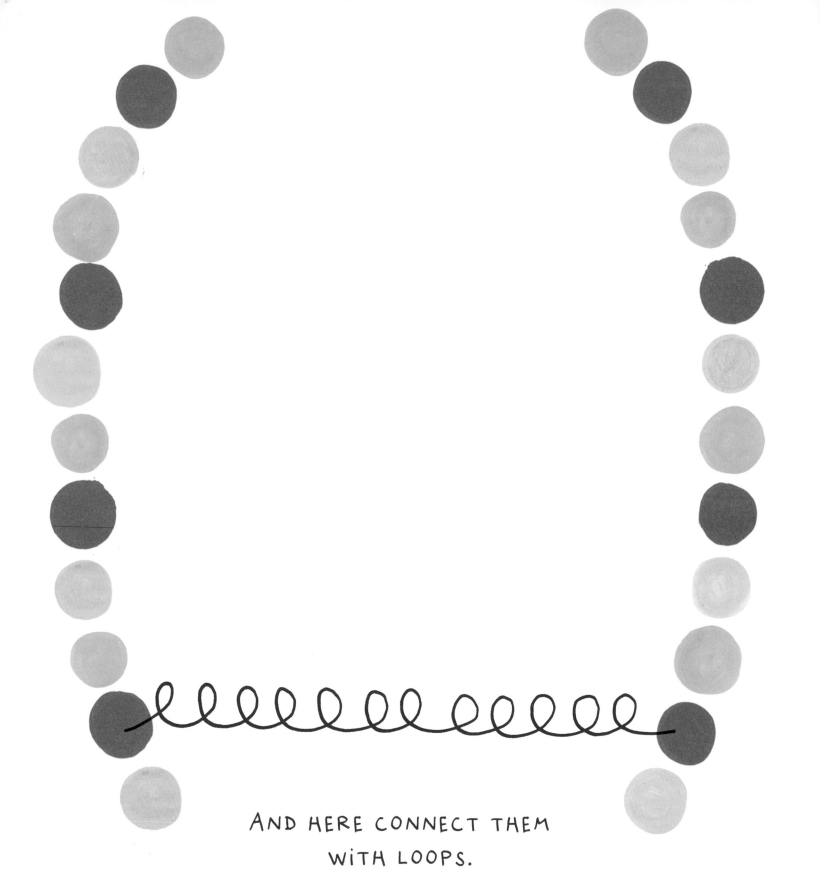

AND HERE CONNECT THEM
WITH LOOPS.

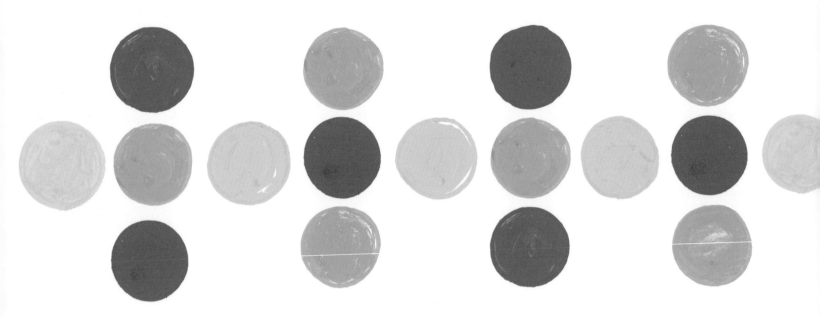

JUMP FROM YELLOW DOT TO YELLOW DOT WITH YOUR CRAYON.

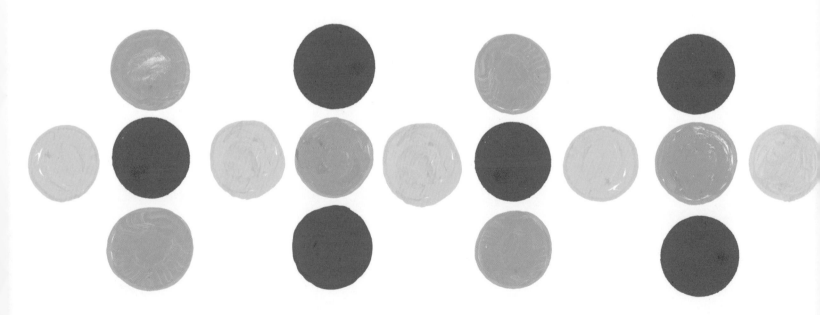

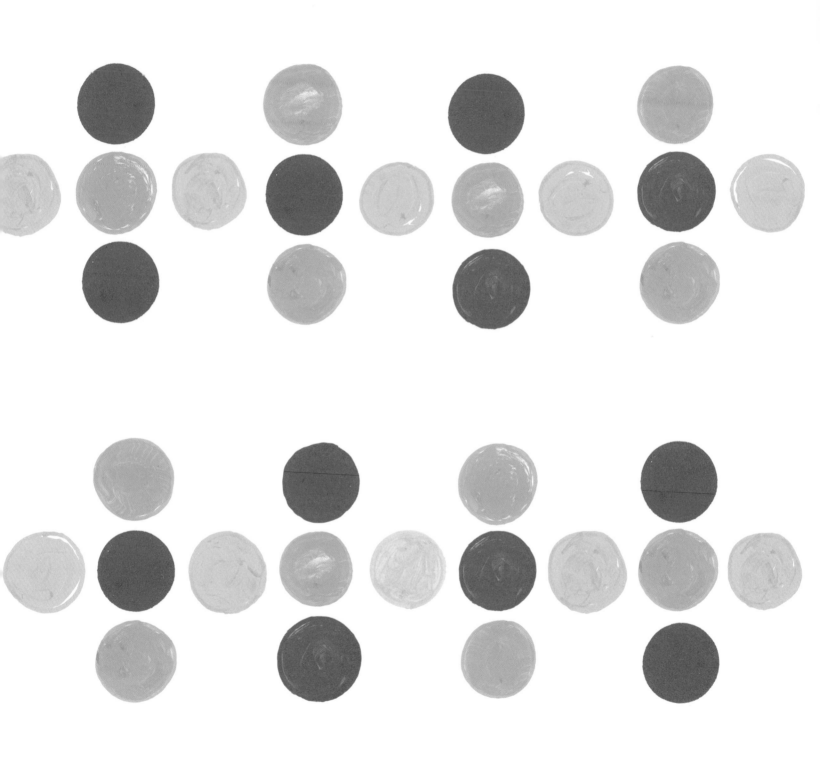

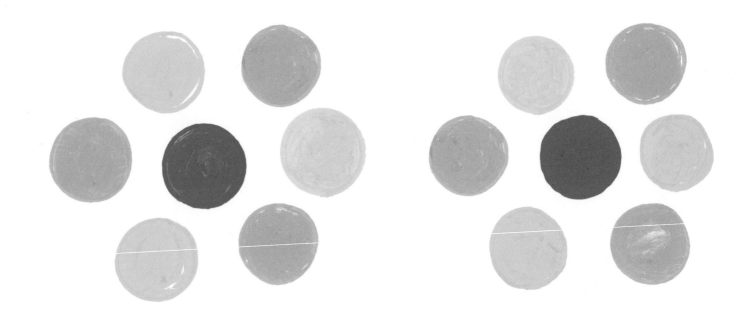

NOW JUMP FROM BLUE DOT TO BLUE DOT
WITH YOUR COLORED PENCIL.

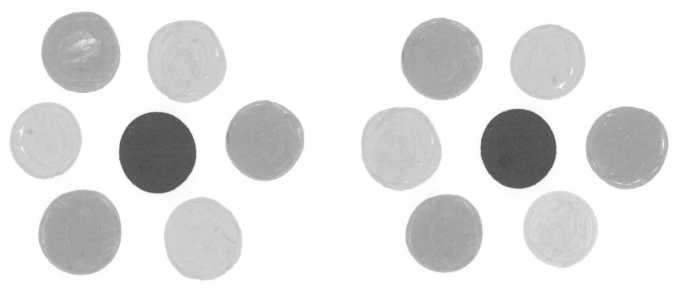

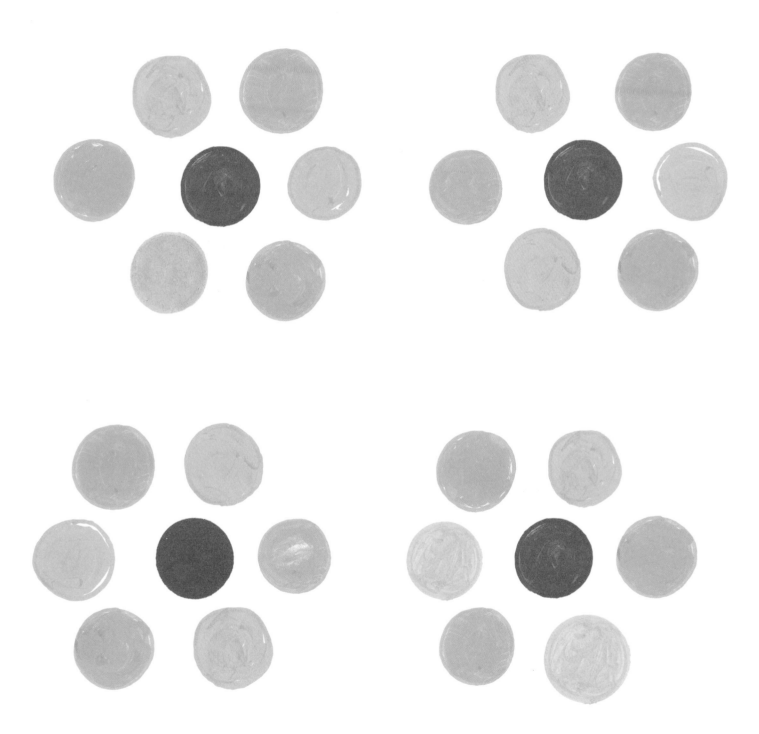

FINALLY, CONNECT ALL THE RED DOTS.

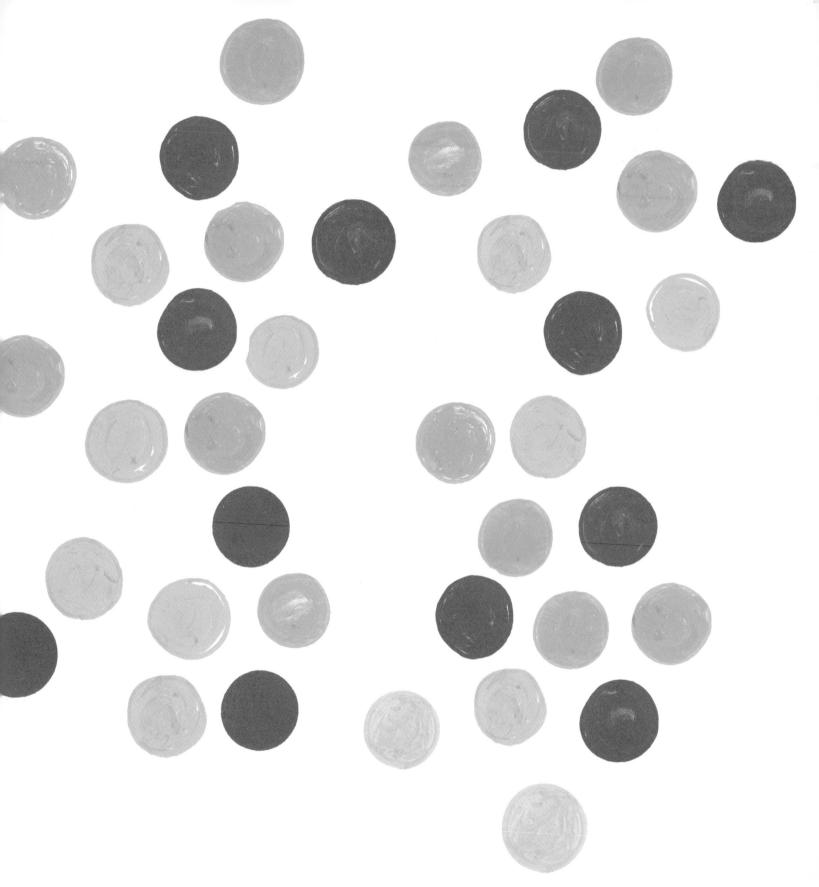

DRAW A PATH FROM
THIS BLACK DOT . . .

TO THIS BLACK DOT
WITHOUT TOUCHING A
SINGLE OTHER DOT!

DRAW AROUND ALL THESE DOTS WITHOUT
TOUCHING ANY OF THEM.

DRAW A PATH FROM ONE SIDE OF THE PAGE TO
THE OTHER BETWEEN THE DOTS.

DRAW AS LONG A PATH AS POSSIBLE WITHOUT
TOUCHING A SINGLE DOT.

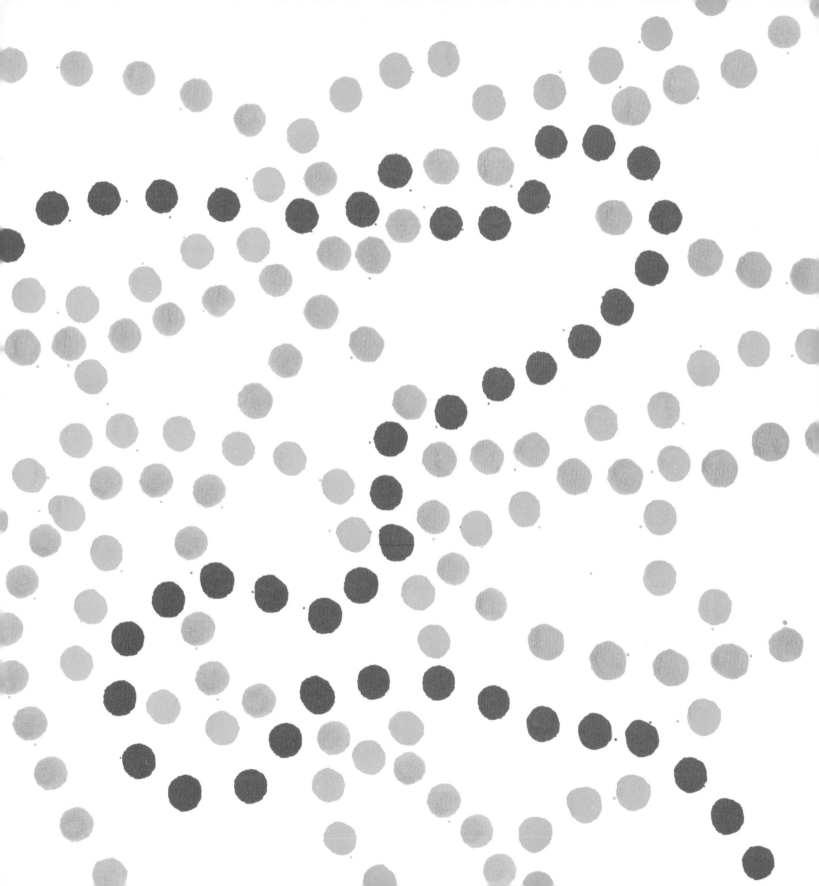

FIND ALL THE DOTS AND DRAW A CIRCLE
AROUND EACH ONE.

NOW FIND ALL THE DOTS HERE AND DRAW
A CIRCLE AROUND EACH ONE.

AND DO IT AGAIN ON THIS PAGE!

DRAW A CIRCLE AROUND EACH GROUP OF DOTS
OF THE SAME COLOR.

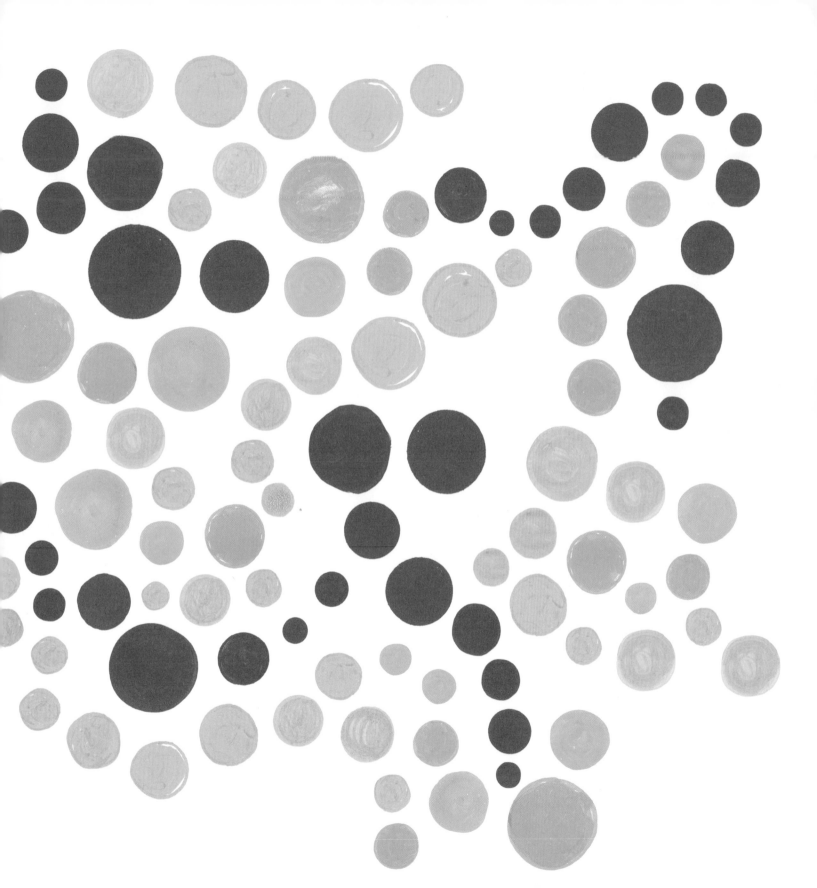

CIRCLE EVERY PAIR OF DOTS . . . TWO BY TWO
BY TWO.

NOW CIRCLE THE DOTS THREE BY THREE
BY THREE.

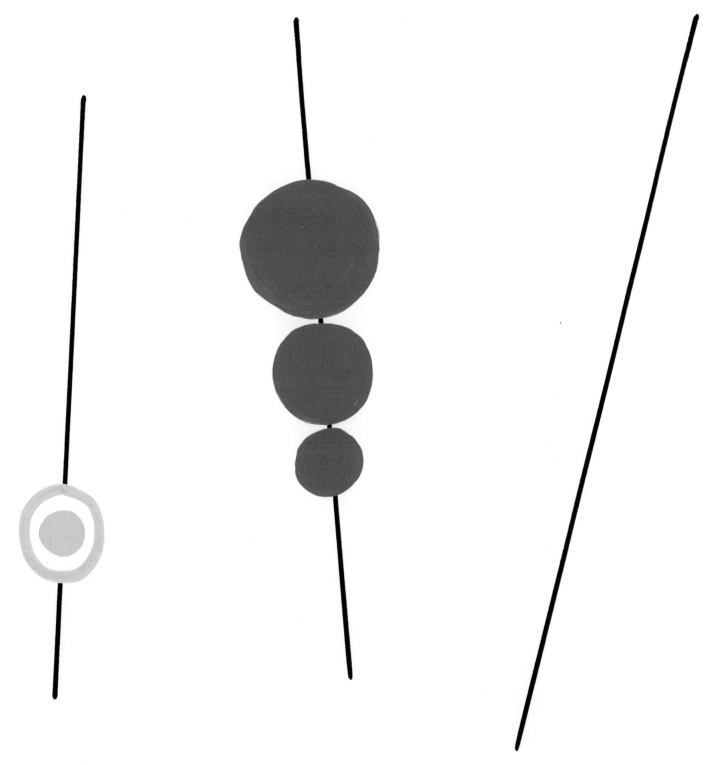

CATCH SOME DOTS ON THESE STICKS.

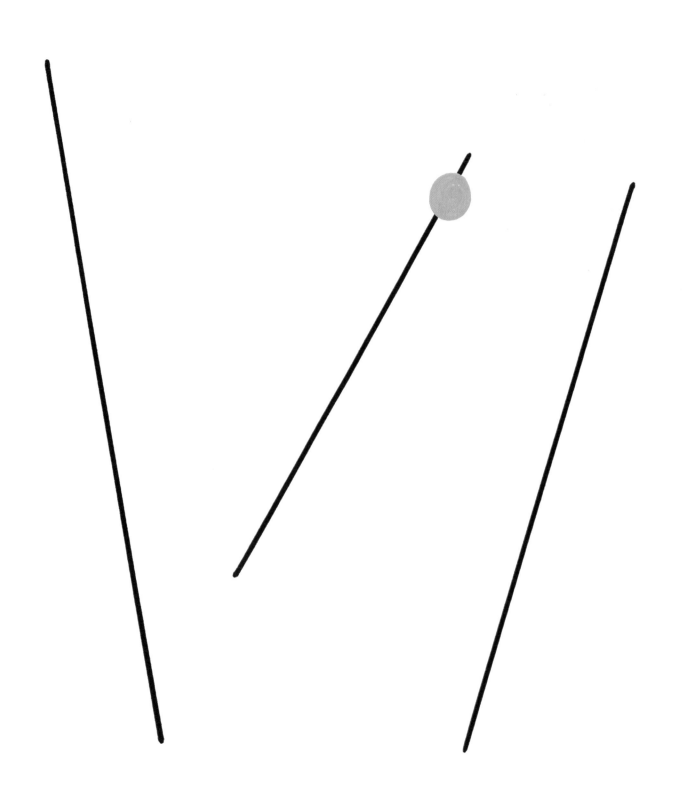

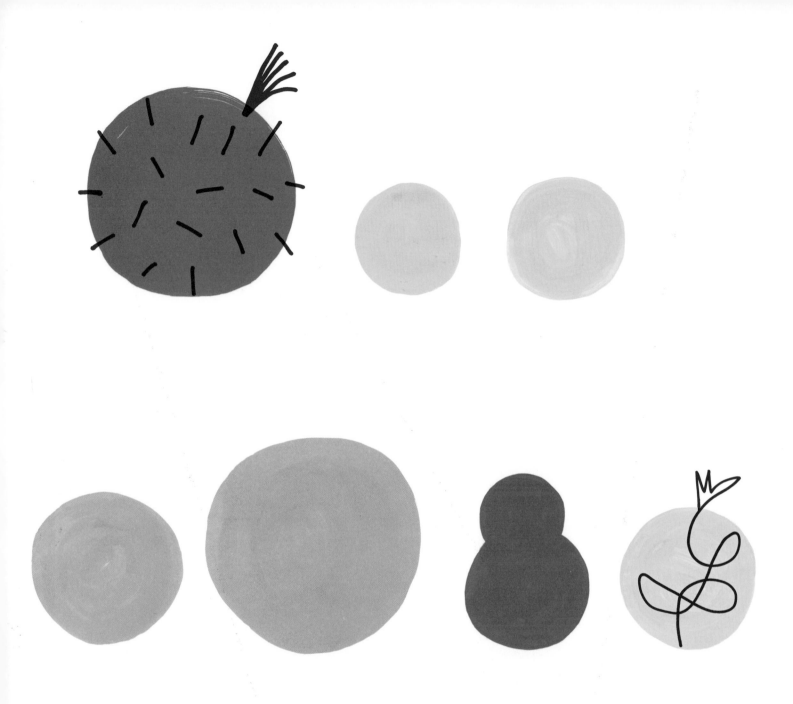

INVENT SOME FUN FRUIT.

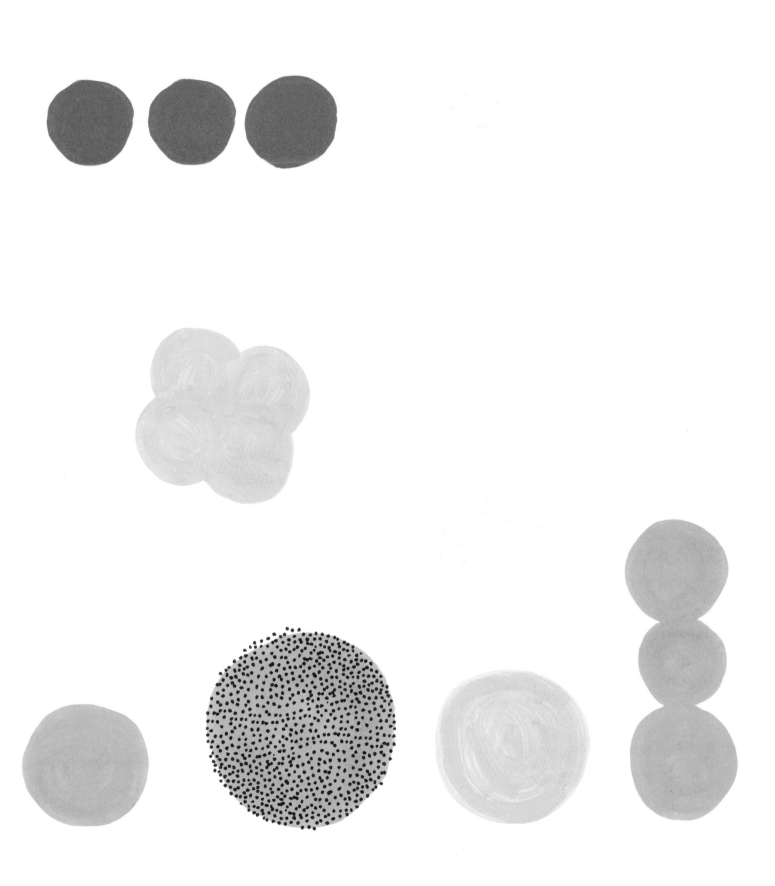

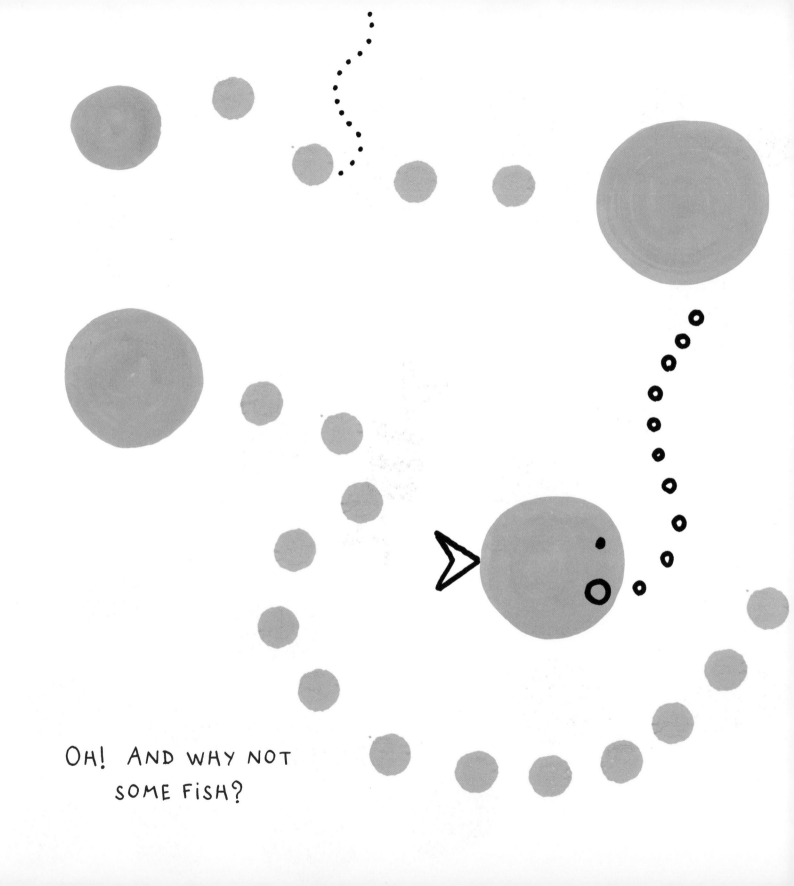

OH! AND WHY NOT
SOME FISH?

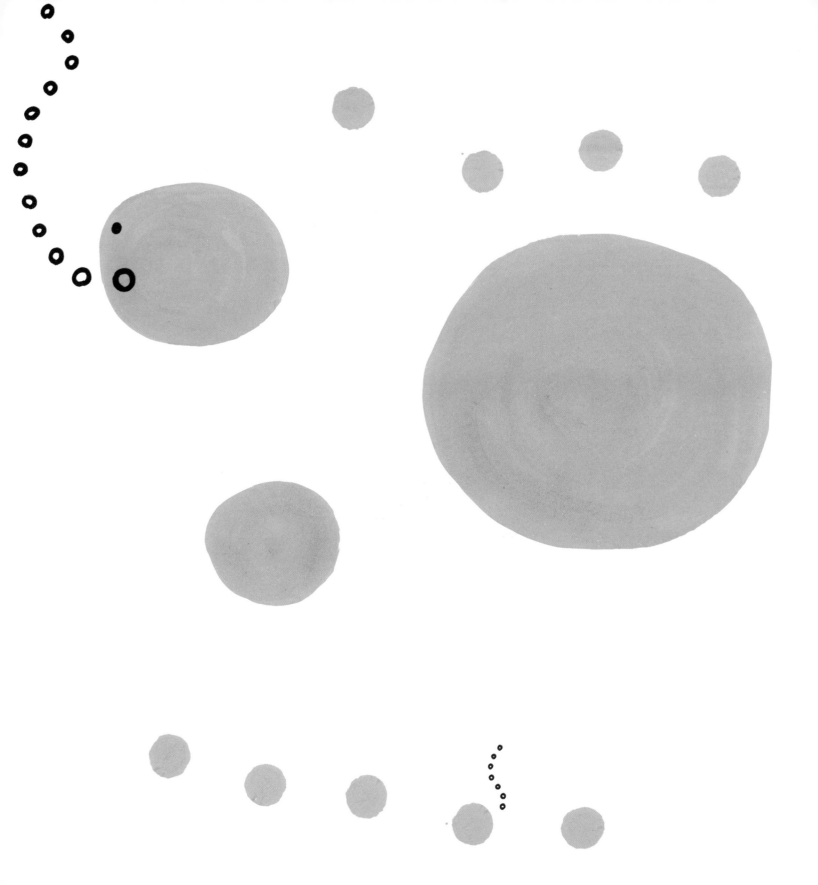

PUT SOME WHEELS ON THOSE CARS

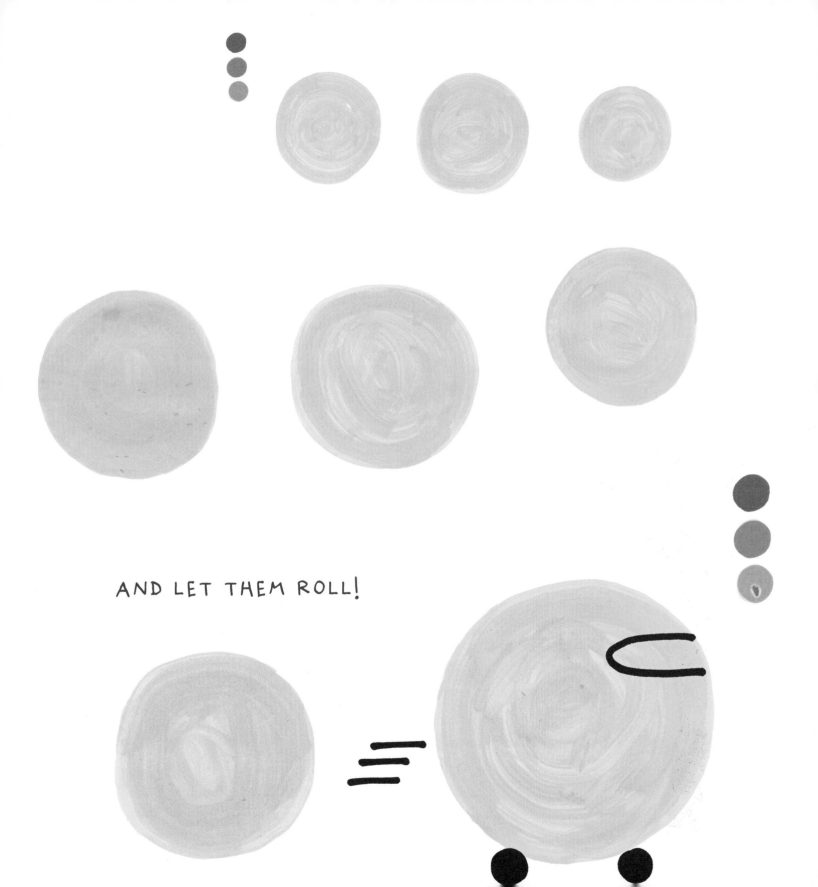

AND LET THEM ROLL!

AND MAKE SOME TREES WITH THESE DOTS . . .

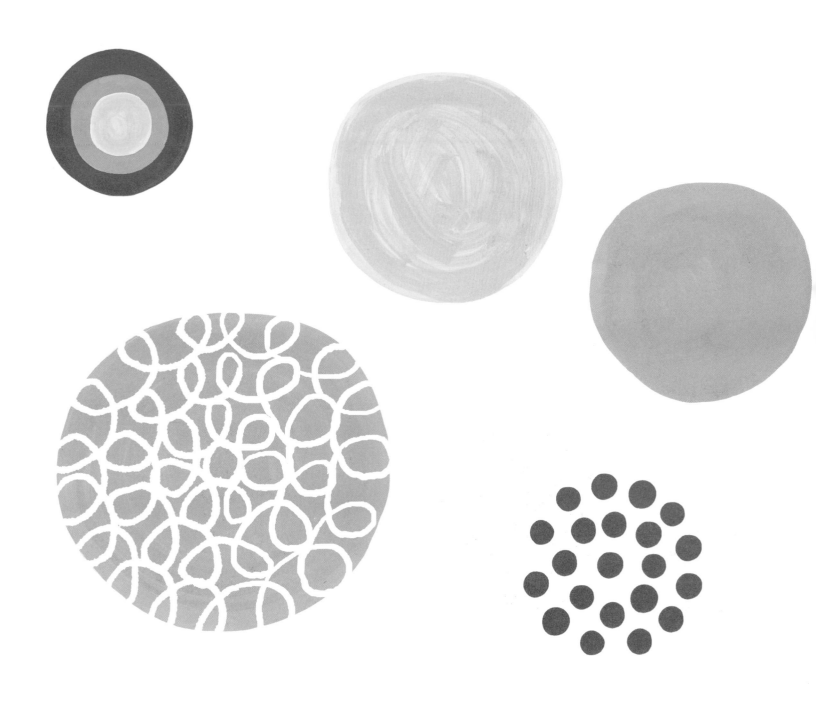

GROW A HUGE FOREST!

WITH THESE DOTS,
MAKE FLOWERS . . .

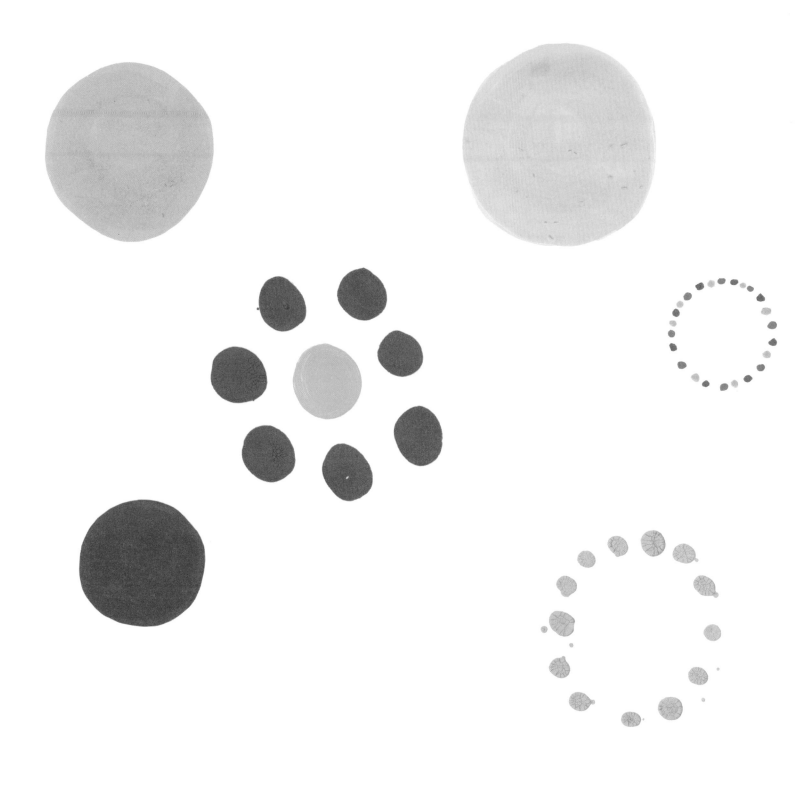

IN FACT, MAKE A WHOLE FIELD FULL OF FLOWERS!

DRAW TWO GIANT BOUQUETS OF DOTS.

THESE DOTS ARE PEOPLE. DRAW AND DISCOVER THEM!

AND FINALLY, THESE DOTS ARE FACES.

DRAW THEM ALL!

First published in the United States of America in 2019 by Handprint/Chronicle Books LLC.
Originally published in France in 2018 by Bayard Éditions under the title "Points Points."

Library of Congress Cataloging-in-Publication Data available.
ISBN 978-1-4521-7860-8

Manufactured in China.

Translated by Christopher Franceschelli.
Original French edition design by Sandrine Granon.
Handprint/Chronicle Books design by Amelia Mack.
Typeset in Hervé Tullet Whimsy.

The illustrations in this book were rendered in paint.
10 9 8 7 6 5 4 3 2 1

Handprint Books
an imprint of Chronicle Books LLC
680 Second Street
San Francisco, California 94107

www.chroniclekids.com

WAY OF THE DOLL

DEDICATION

This book is dedicated to my mother, who always supported the artist in me, and to my beloved children: Emerald, Lauren, and Caitlyn, who encouraged me to re-create my dreams in reality.

WAY OF THE DOLL

THE ART AND CRAFT OF PERSONAL TRANSFORMATION

Cassandra Light

To Carolyn;
My Dear Friend and Inspiring Teacher.
Love,
Linda
1998

Foreword by
Stephen Mitchell

Essay by
Jean Shinoda Bolen

CHRONICLE BOOKS
SAN FRANCISCO

ACKNOWLEDGMENTS

Printed in Hong Kong.

Book and cover design: Susan Verba
Cover photograph: Kevin Ng

Library of Congress Cataloging-in-Publication Data:
Light, Cassandra
Way of the doll / by Cassandra Light.
p. cm.
ISBN 0-8118-0698-7
1. Self-disclosure—Case studies.
2. Catharsis—Case studies.
3. Dolls—Psychological aspects.
4. Symbolism in art.
5. Mental healing.
I. Title
BF697.5.S427L54 1995
158—dc20   94-48177
                                                    CIP

Excerpt from *The Pregnant Virgin* by Marion Woodman used with permission from Inner City Books, © 1985.

Excerpt from *Eros and Pathos* by Aldo Carotenuto used with permission from Inner City Books, © 1989.

Excerpt from *Rodin* by Rainer Maria Rilke used with permission from Peregrine Smith Books, © 1979.

Excerpt from *The Selected Poetry of Rainer Maria Rilke*, edited and translated by Stephen Mitchell, used with permission from Random House/Vintage Books, © 1980, 1981, 1982.

Distributed in Canada by Raincoast Books,
8680 Cambie Street
Vancouver, B.C., V6P 6M9

10 9 8 7 6 5 4 3 2 1

Chronicle Books
275 Fifth St.
San Francisco, CA 94103

I want to acknowledge Sammael Gromowsky whose creative vision and unwavering support made the Doll Show, the doll process, and this book possible. I also want to thank Patrick Finley, who has inspired me in more ways than I could ever express and whose writing and editing have shaped my words into poetry. And I want to thank Richard Glantz, whose clarity has tempered my wild imagination into reality. I also want to offer my special gratitude to Nion McEvoy at Chronicle Books, whose humor and friendship guided me through what I thought was an impossible task—making a book. I would like to thank Barbara Traub Stuart and Liz Clark, for their unconditional receptivity, which supported and nurtured my creative process. And finally, a special thanks to Meghan Adkins, who, in the end, put together all the bits and pieces.

I would also like to acknowledge my mentors: Marion Woodman, Maria Von Franz, Jean Houston, T. S. Eliot, and Rainer Maria Rilke, whose books have contributed greatly to the alchemy of our times. And finally I want to acknowledge all my students—past, present, and future—who have taught me everything I know about soul-making, art, and transformation.

Table of Contents

Sometimes I think that the creation of a work of art is the most mysterious process in the world. "The Lord formed a human from the clay of the ground and blew into its nostrils the breath of life, and the human became a living being." Without that breath all imaginable skill is nothing, and the clay remains clay—beautiful to look at, perhaps, but incapable of touching and transforming us in our depths.

I have known Cassandra Light's work for almost ten years now, and from the beginning I was startled by its aliveness. The first doll of hers that I fell in love with was the figure of a Zen Master:

> *Three feet tall, he sits cross-legged inside a wooden frame in a corner of the living room. He isn't aware of me as I tiptoe closer. Shhh. Leaning over the page, intensely seeing, he rests his left arm on one black-robed knee and lets the small black ritual bib dangle from his neck. So much love in this white porcelain face with its network of glaze-cracks, so much suffering digested and transformed into wisdom. His ink-stained porcelain hands, like two small sea-animals, seem to have eyes at the end of each finger. He has just finished drawing a circle, letting the dark ink thin out as his brush moves around the rice paper, until at the end (the beginning) there is only a faintly brushed trace of it, the mark of a mind running on empty. As for the circle's meaning: Unity? Completion? Nirvana? Give me a break.*
>
> *He looks down at his handiwork, as I look down at him, satisfied and on the brink of amusement. The mouth doesn't show even the trace of a smile. But the smile is there, somewhere, shining in the heaven of his face like a new moon.*
>
> (from *Parables and Portraits*, HarperCollins, 1990)

Then there was her Turtle Master, green and wrinkled and soul-wise, a kind of reptilian Yoda. And the two dolls in Psyche's Journey—the boatman and the pale abstracted young woman whose whole body speaks of her vast death, which, in Rilke's words, is so new to her, she cannot understand that it has happened. And, over the years, there were many others.

Each of these dolls is an embodiment of psychic truth. Each one breathes with the breath of life, and therefore has the power to transform us, as its maker was transformed in the making. The Way of the Doll, like all creative paths, leads both inside and outside, since the way up and the way down are one and the same. And as with all genuine practices, the only criterion is wholeheartedness. "Thus in our practice of Buddhism," Dogen wrote (for *Buddhism* you can substitute *awareness*), "when we master one truth, we master all truths; and when we complete one activity, we complete all activities. The place is here; the way leads everywhere."

Stephen Mitchell

Essay

"You must go see *The Way of the Doll*. You have to go yourself to get why; I cannot explain it." Words followed, like "mythic," "symbolic," "powerful." When a second and third woman urged me to see this exhibit, I made it over. It was across the bay from where I live, in a space the size of a small mom and pop grocery store in an industrial section of town. The next year, the exhibit was larger, housed for the time in a series of interconnected rooms which made viewing it a labyrinthine experience. The exhibit grew into warehouse spaces next. Each exhibit not only drew more people to them, they drew more people—mostly women but some men as well—into Cassandra Light's *The Way of the Doll* classes. I learned through them of the psychological and creative process that drew stunning work out of them. They created life-size figures that went beyond expectations of their own artistic ability, and each doll was inbued with soul, which made their work, and the exhibit, an experience akin to meeting dream figures.

With an eye for the visual arts which has drawn me to museums, exhibits, and having an art-filled home and office, there is an aesthetic I appreciate in Cassandra's work and in the exhibit in general that is fine art. It is not this dimension that I am either qualified to comment on or have something to say about, however. It is, instead, my particular perspective as a Jungian analyst and author of books such as *Goddesses in Everywoman* and *Gods in Everyman* in which I describe how personal psychology and archetypal patterns come together in us to shape who we are and what issues we may be fated to meet in our lives.

Entering the exhibit of *The Way of the Doll* is an encounter with powerful archetypal figures shaped, garbed, and often placed in settings that came out of the symbolic psyche of each participant in the "doll class." On crossing the threshold into the exhibit, viewers enter the symbolic realm. We encounter inner figures, figures remembered from the past, figures from powerful dreams, active imagination, or myths. There is often a resemblance between a doll and its creator, which is fitting, because the personal and archetypal come together in each work. When anyone gives shape and form to archtypal experience, the work will reverberate in the psyche of others, because we all share a collective unconscious which accounts for the impact of these dolls. A particular doll made by one person may express a memory, a dream, or a life experience of the viewer.

The doll's creator is invited to write something about the doll for the exhibit. In the writing, the viewer of the exhibit gets an insight into the psychological process out of which the doll grew. Many class sessions are not about creating the doll as an object at all, but instead serve to activate the contents of the psyche. Classes become a safe place to share deeply personal stories. Healing occurs when we can talk of what we did or what was done to us or what we witnessed and have kept secret, out of shame and pain. To then make a doll that reflects these wounds transforms the experience for the creator, and the work has an authenticity that invites viewers to be touched as deeply as the creator went in their own process.

When a group or another person or therapist can be trusted with parts of ourselves that are wounded, that same safety makes it possible for new, vulnerable, innocent parts of a person to emerge, as well as becoming a place to share valued parts of one's inner life that have not been expressed elsewhere. For work such as I have seen in the exhibit, I know that these classes had to be a sanctuary, a sacred place. Depth work is not just about wounds and pain, but about discovering sources of creativity and spirituality; about finding the beauty of one's own soul and having it seen and valued by others. In the exhibit, there are dolls that express all of these qualities.

I see *The Way of the Doll* as an expression of Cassandra Light's gift as an artist who taps into the archetypal layer of the psyche to bring forth not only her own work, but the psyche and work of others. I have long felt that depth therapy is an art form; through work done in Cassandra Light's doll classes, I see that an art form can also be depth therapy.

Jean Shinoda Bolen, M. D.

Cassandra Light
Photo by Margo Weinstein

"If you find it possible, return now with a portion of your weaned and grown-up feelings to any of your childhood things, one which you always had with you. Think whether there was ever anything closer, more intimate or more necessary to you than such a thing. Whether everything else was not in a position to harm you or to be unfair, to frighten you with pain or to bewilder you with uncertainty? If you found kindness in your first experiences, and trust and companionship, wasn't this because of it? Wasn't it a thing with which you shared your little heart, like a piece of bread that must be large enough for two?"

—Rainer Maria Rilke

WHY WE CALL THEM DOLLS

The images and writings in this book were not created by professional artists. They were made by ordinary people involved in an extraordinary process—artistic, psychological, and spiritual—that has evolved over fifteen years at Way of the Doll School of Sacred Art in Berkeley, California. Since I began the school, many people have tried to convince me to call the figures in these images something other than *dolls*. Some have told me the work would be better understood if I used a term like *archetypes* or *mythic figures*. Several of my students have spoken of their difficulty in communicating to others just what a *doll*, in our context, is. Though there are many intricately woven threads of psychology, mythology, and art therapy involved in the process I teach, the term *doll* has a special and precise meaning for us.

My colleagues and I insist on this term because our teachings are rooted in the mythic landscape of childhood, and dolls carry childhood dreams. Words like *sculptures* or *icons* evoke the art world of adults, of aesthetics, philosophy, and commerce. *Dolls* conjures instead the world we lived in as children. A place where a beloved plaything spoke in the voice of a guardian angel; where, in a fearful moment, we held tightly to some precious doll or stuffed bear to ward off the bogey man hiding in the dark.

Myths and archetypes, rituals and complexes are adult explanations of psychic realities experienced in our earliest years. Dolls, as objects of our creative imagination, will, if we invite them, take us to play again in the house of our childhood past and perhaps bestow upon us a future we hadn't imagined. That past is where the journey to a new future through the Way of the Doll begins.

Still Dancer
55 in., 1992
Nancy Foster, Attorney-Mediator

This book is not a how-to book about doll making, nor is it an addition to, nor a substitute for, any therapeutic process. It is an illustration of a journey made by individuals. A student enters my class with a need to change or transform something in his or her life. The people who are my students are neither with nor without problems, not necessarily happy or unhappy. By making a doll within a creative circle made up of other people, they begin to discover their own stories in the shapes they are forming, and they continue to retell that story to the others. Their stories of past wounding and betrayal, of loneliness and hope, reveal a common desire: to be reunited in the original unconditional love of a parent, to be acknowledged and accepted. It is a desire that at some time in their pasts was thwarted or blocked, and through acts of memory, ritual, and creativity they seek to fulfill. The external vessel of this fulfillment, the record of its coming into being, is the doll.

The Way of the Doll centers around the creation of an actual doll. The doll is made in many ways, through a melding of many processes that will be described later in this book. Most importantly, we make the doll from clay, and we build it from the feet up. We create the feet first to learn the stages of clay and to sense how we stand in the world, where our center ground is and where our hopes and fears are rooted. The foot reflects these feelings back to us—both as desires and limitations—and so becomes, in the material world, our first teacher.

Once our feelings and attitudes have become somewhat revealed, we find we need more guidance and so create, literally, a face; a face meant to show us what we need to see. Then, in order to grasp this new understanding and to fashion the emerging image of ourselves, we need to have hands. Finally, as our new knowledge transforms us and reveals itself in full body and story, we create the costume, the name, the tale and, in the end, the scene and

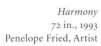

Harmony
72 in., 1993
Penelope Fried, Artist

written statement that completes the outward manifestation of what has been a year-long journey. That final manifestation is what you see in the photographs in this book.

Like a new student to my class, I want you as the reader to begin with a certain sense of mystery, with the understanding that this book is about a very unique and complex process and so must, to be accurate, proceed in an equally unique and complex way. To describe how these images came into being and what they represent, evocation, imagery, anecdote, and poetry are all necessary. These *dolls* are like seeds in that they contain all the processes—rational, imaginative, conscious, and unconscious—that later evolve into separate parts: art, science, pragmatism, and spirituality, but are in the beginning united in what, for children, is the basic experience of play. To be reunited, feeling to thinking, breathing to speaking, waking to dreaming, the conscious and unconscious brought together in a dance, is the song that the dolls sing to all who listen. In the doll's eyes, we are all children again, all part of the circle. We need only to be reconnected, as our earliest playthings or special objects connected us to the vast outside world by teaching us how to share our "little heart, like a piece of bread that must be large enough for two."

"Modern men and women, pulled by the same magnet that drew Ice Age man up to the cave, are journeying through the dark labyrinth of their own souls. In spite of the pain and terror involved, the archetype of the way lures them; they yearn to bring the unconscious into consciousness. Penetrating into that tunnel of death and potential rebirth demands supreme effort, tenaciously holding on with no conscious orientation until a light shines in the darkness. Only if the tension between the anxiety and the fascination is held, will the combustion point occur—the point where the tearing apart ceases and a sense of unity is experienced. And with this unity there invariably comes an image."

—Marion Woodman

Persephone (left), 46 in., 1992
Eros (below), 40 in., 1990
Cassandra Light

1

In the Spirit of Re-Creation

CASSANDRA'S TALE

"I don't create the doll, the doll creates me."

There was a woman who had a beloved, but broken-hearted father. When she was three years old, he died of heart failure. This was a great loss, but the greater loss was that her mother, who was very young, unsupported, and misguided, told her that her father had just gone away.

I was that little girl. For a great part of my life I waited for my father to come back. My sorrow and longing were often so painful that, to assuage it, I began to make things in clay and invent worlds where I might be reunited with him. In time, as my heart and life grew older, his memory became that of a distant but much-loved god. Sometimes he would take the form of a humanitarian ideal and I would dream that the purpose of my life was to feed the hungry or give sanctuary to lost children. In contrast to such dreams, my actual childhood was a dark place of great loneliness. The world I lived in with my mother, stepfather, and two brothers was profoundly different from the one I carried inside me. As in most families, where secrets and sorrows pull relentlessly at truth and joy, everyone was acted upon by an underworld of unconscious action. We each inflicted on one another some form of harm molded in the fire of our own suffering.

This is where I believe the seed of my own soul making began: in having had a great love, losing that love to death, having that death hidden, and then spending my life searching for and uncovering what is hidden in love. In this quest, I found the process of making art to be the only family that loved me unconditionally. Making things and dreaming impossible dreams kept my excruciating longing contained, while seeking to become an artist led me to teachers who protected and honored my gifts. To these teachers I have given my gratitude by becoming a teacher myself.

How I was guided onto a spiritual path and became a teacher is another story. It begins when I moved to Berkeley, twenty-three years ago. I arrived at eighteen and immediately felt as if I'd awoken from a nightmare into a place where my dreams could come true. The means and the people were all present for my emergence. But I found I was severely limited in my education. I lacked worldly confidence and was psychologically damaged. It was fortunate that I arrived where and when I did. Here, in this unique place, I encountered every kind of therapy. I attended an alternative university which supported my self-directed learning. I began to discover the healing aspects of art, ritual, and theater. And, most importantly, I acquired a transpersonal perspective by being exposed to feminist spirituality, alchemy, and the Goddess. This larger view of humanity expanded my own personal story and, in turn, my own world view. In Berkeley, the limited family of my childhood was replaced by a larger tribe or community. These experiences began to shape what has come to be the philosophy behind The Way of the Doll.

When I was twenty-one I had a daughter. In a sense, the two of us grew up together. Like my mother, I was thrust into responsibility at an early age and forced to find a way to survive. It seemed that I was destined at that point, being immersed in the educational process as I was, to pursue teaching as a profession. Because I didn't have traditional teaching credentials, I was going to have to create my own school. This turned out to be a blessing. My lack of conventional training forced me to rely on my inner world, a world basically driven by my desire to reunite with my lost father. This unconscious drive inspired me to teach art spiritually, as a healing practice. Since I had no actual teachers to guide me in this specific form, I had to use myself and my own story as the example. I discovered that my passion to find and transform what was hidden in my own psyche was the best teacher and guide I could have had. It gave me the courage and foolish wisdom I needed to travel in my own way. But it was also clear that I needed others to explore and impart their own experiences along that way. I needed people to mirror my story just as they needed mine to mirror theirs. What I was seeking was a path toward self-transformation. What I discovered was that, for me, such a path was best traveled in a group. And in that discovery, without my even realizing it, the doll school began.

Doll Story Theater, 1986
Françoise Papon and
Arina Isaacson
Photo by Janet Cole

HISTORY OF THE SCHOOL

I began to understand, from my experiences as a young woman artist, what part of the artistic process was clearly magical and transforming. This led me to a particular kinship with clay. Because clay can take the shape of unformed thoughts and feelings, it allows the maker to transform an unconscious state of mind to a conscious one. After a time I began to add feathers, sticks, and cloth to my clay work, and what emerged were fetish-like dolls. I became increasingly interested in making masks and magical charms. In 1979, I was commissioned by a local patron of the arts to make a fortune-teller doll. The power and energy this doll emanated threw me into a state of great confusion. I was so uncertain about what I had created that I went to a psychic. She told me that I had access to realms of great knowledge and power, but, if I didn't want to get into trouble with this power, I needed to ground it in a spiritual practice. The only spiritual experience I had any real connection with at that point was that of the Goddess and the old pagan tradition, worshiping nature and her seasonal influences, so I gathered together a group of women whose purpose it was to create a ritual circle loosely based on what I understood of this religion. Not long after this, I was approached by a group of nine women interested in making charms, amulets, and fetishes. Because of my work in mask and theater and my experience with the fortune-teller doll, I proposed a class in which we would make performing dolls. In the fall of 1980, we began creating what we thought of as a ritual-doll theater.

Each week the women made doll parts out of clay. Like most of the students who have followed this first class, they had never really made art before. As beginners, and because we were more focused on ritual then on making artifacts, it took an entire year to complete the first class. Yet together we intuitively created a process. At the end of that year we introduced our dolls in a theater piece at the Berkeley Art Center. This was the first Doll Show.

Brilliance
9 in., 1993
Cassandra Light

I did not, at the time, expect to teach another doll class. But to my surprise, nine more women asked me to lead a new circle, and so we continued to explore the doll work together.

Over the years the process has evolved because of who has traveled with it. Every person who comes and goes makes his or her unique contribution. When therapists joined the process, they invested it with their own psychology; Jungians made it Jungian; Buddhists made it Buddhistic; artists, poets, ritualists, and storytellers have all offered their gifts. So, as the circles continued, the process developed. Now, fifteen years later, we are a school of seventy year-long students, with two teachers (Sam Gromowsky and myself) and five assistants. Our dolls and shows have grown to such magnitude that we need a gigantic display space, and our reputation brings thousands of viewers to the Doll Show each year.

As the process and the dolls have evolved, so has the way in which we think about them. In the beginning we thought of them as performing dolls, to be used and acted upon in a kind of ritual theater. We knew that they were more than mere dolls, that they were part of a larger story. We saw that they embodied our ancestors, our tribes, our dreams and illustrated the myths and stories of the archetypes. Today, after fifteen years of refining the process, we gaze upon those stories not as theatrical events acted out in time, but as precisely fashioned narrative tableaux, fixed in a single frame. This is what you see in the photographs in this book. It's as if one took a single image to represent all the actions that preceded and will succeed it: Psyche, at the moment she is about to turn the light upon her husband Eros, is fixed as a figure in eternity, embodying her entire story up to that moment, while also containing, in that single, startling image, everything that is to come.

Longing
39 in., 1992
Cassandra Light

The Compassionate Mother

In telling my original wounding story, I spoke mostly about the loss of my father. But the other essential loss was the psychic or symbolic loss of my mother. She, like many others of her generation, suffered from a lack of real mothering, as did her mother before her. Not having been taught the wisdom of the feminine, she could not use it to nourish her own children, and so contributed, despite her best intentions, to the ongoing story of the Abandoning Mother.

Since the beginning of time, women have sat in circles making things and telling stories. They have sewed, shaped, and woven their joys and sorrows into many a handicraft. Telling stories and making things together helped them make sense of their world. It was through these unacknowledged crafts passed down by families and clans, that the real truth of a woman's life and of those who listened to her was kept. These traditions are still extant. But in order to receive their wisdom, which is the wisdom of the feminine, we must gather together and renew the basic forms of feminine art—art that teaches the language of relatedness, of love, and of clan. The lack of this has left many of us now impoverished of soul and hungry for the old healing circles.

But these healing circles are not confined to women. Proof of this is apparent as each year more and more men enter the doll process. They see an art form at the Doll Show invested with a meaning and collaborative connection different from that of the masculine, a form that balances and completes their knowledge. In the context of ritual creativity and storytelling, they are invited to play with dolls. And they do so. In discovering their own doll story, they recognize the possibility of restoring the more receptive, feminine side of their personalities. Presently there are classes at the school with almost as many men as women, and it is my experience that the tone and quality of these circles has only improved as a result. Many times, after getting into the process a bit, a man will find himself explaining quite naturally to his male friends that "he's off to his doll class now." This might raise an eyebrow or two but most men come to appreciate the courage it takes to open up personally and share vulnerable aspects of themselves.

Whether man or woman, young or old, we all share a need for compassionate mothering. By exchanging our stories, circle members discovered that this great need was going largely unfulfilled in our society. We realized that we, as a tribe of motherless children, were going to have to re-create the Compassionate Mother for each other. We came to understand that what bound us together was a powerful human desire for connectedness. We were all unconsciously longing for the loving embrace of a mother who loves us above all. So together we have formed collective circles to remember and celebrate the essential wisdom of compassionate mothering. For it is in compassion that we reconnect to each other—and to the world.

La Luna
16.5 in., 1992
Dahlia Kamesar, Tax Preparer/Writer

Anthos, 60 in., 1990
Sprite, 18 in., 1991
Sukey Wilder, Systems Analyst

2

Keeping the Channel Open

Many people have stopped believing they have anything of value in them worth expressing. "Maybe artists do" they say, "but not me. And even if I did, who would appreciate it?" I believe, like Martha Graham, that each of us has a unique voice. And when any voice is stifled by an inner tyrant or outer critic, the full chorus of humanity is diminished. But, once we find time in our busy lives to explore and create our own expressions, and if we do this with kindred souls, then all things become possible.

You might say that I am dreaming. I would say that is exactly what we need to do. This book is a testament to such dreaming. Our intention in this book is to weave a tapestry of images and stories that we hope will inspire you. The people who created these images did not think of themselves as artists when they entered the process. By the time they finished they had a new definition of the term "making art." It is our sincere hope that their written and sculpted expressions will encourage you to take the same challenge.

FORMING THE CLASS

A man once wrote me a letter a couple of months after he'd seen a Doll Show. In it he expressed extreme gratitude. He was eighty years old and had recently experienced a stroke, leaving him somewhat paralyzed in his right hand. In his youth he had been a classical musician, but had given up playing the piano to become a family man. He came to the show one afternoon and was profoundly moved by the courage and hope that emanated from the dolls. The dollmakers and their stories invited him to follow his heart's desire. He went home in tears, found a music teacher, and began to train his left hand to do what his right hand could no longer attempt. In his letter he expressed to me his child-like wonder: It was not too late to try the impossible.

Vulture Mother
48 in., 1992
Pamela Pierson

Psyche
48 in., 1990
Padma Catell, Psychologist

There are also times when someone's friend or relative, unprepared to see their own pain, judges the show to be a house of horrors. They leave feeling fearful and closed off to the possiblity that these images, although sometimes dark and frightening, contain the shadow of their maker while the maker, him- or herself, has moved on.

More often than not, what happened to the eighty-year-old man occurs. People come to the show and are entranced. They willingly participate in this waking dream and have an experience of what it is like to be guided. For that is what the doll should be: a guide within you—or that guide's teaching—made outwardly manifest.

24

The S.A.S.H.A. of Compassion (Self-Affirming, Soul-Healing Africans)
51 in., 1993
Taj Johns, Assistant Management Analyst

Motherlove
48 in., 1992
Edith L. Murphy, Physical Therapist

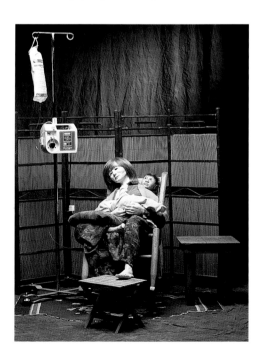

Most people who join the classes do so because a particular doll touched them. They may have always wanted to create but were never given the necessary encouragement or support. In one startling moment a certain doll's story gave them the courage to believe that they too could become dollmakers.

Sometimes artists come to the show, the spark of inspiration having died inside them. They see in the doll process the possibility of getting their creativity back on track, so they join us.

There are also those who recognize in the show an inspired and loving expression of community support. Suddenly they are struck by how isolated their lives have become. They sense in the doll tableaux something larger than mere individual creation; they sense a collective energy, and are drawn to the idea of a supportive circle.

And finally with some people an old grief resurfaces: someone gone forever but whose loss has yet to be accepted. They remember the grief but have yet to discover its meaning. To their surprise they feel compelled now to make a commitment. In some cases they actually create a memorial doll for a beloved child, spouse, or parent. These are often the dolls that bring an entire class together.

Whatever the specific motivation, most people join the circle because they sense in themselves a possibility of creating something out of their own life experience. When this possibility becomes rooted in their heart, and when their desire grows strong enough, they decide to do something they never thought they would do: They join our circle and stop saying "too late."

"Show me: how the seed is not the fruit

and yet they share a single growth;

how the two is not the one,

and how the one contains them both."

—Patrick Finley

Raizel: Ancestral Spirit
54 in., 1992
Roslyn Tunis, Curator/Consultant

HOLDING UP THE SUN

The doll circles are founded on one basic teaching: Everyone who enters, no matter where they are creatively or spiritually, will aspire to the highest level. If, for instance, I possess the greatest skill in sculpting, everyone will try to rise toward my level. If, however, another dollmaker enters, more developed than myself, then we will all try to rise toward that person's level.

Obviously the question is: How do we insure that such a "rising" occurs? The answer is: By consciously striving toward a collective attitude. We are always seeking to cultivate, through a variety of methods and rituals, an atmosphere of non-competitiveness. If everyone encourages everyone else's success, then this success supports and encourages us all. We do not judge and we do not leave anyone behind. If I feel I need to be better (or worse) than everyone else, then my attitude infects the group. Everyone reacts to my feeling, and we all begin to sink to a lower level. This is why the circle, and the collective feeling of trust and support it nurtures, is essential to any individual doll's coming into being.

This becomes particularly noticeable in the last three months of the class. For in order to complete the immense task of putting on the Doll Show, our emphasis must turn from individual exploration to group effort. If one or two people remain selfishly focused on their own needs, then the group is hindered. It is this very pragmatic attitude of interconnectedness that encourages individuals to mature and discover in themselves a need, even a joy, in acting towards others with honor and integrity. It is announced often and to everyone in the final months: "No one is finished until everyone is finished!"

Earth Father Sky Mother
Male, 60 in.; Female, 36 in., 1993
Barbara Traub Stuart, Investor

As the Pueblo Indians would say: It takes every single person to hold up the sun. If you
don't feel like getting out of bed today, then your part of the sun goes unsupported and the
world suffers from this darkness. We are all neccesary to this world and at some point in
our lives we have to make a hero(ine)'s journey to find this out. To be a hero(ine) is to be
an ordinary person who accomplishes extraordinary things.

"At nyght was come into that hostelrye

Well nyne and twenty in a compagnye

Of sondry folke, by aventure yfallle

In felaweshipe, and pilgrimes were they alle,

That toward Caunterbury wolden ryde."

—Chaucer

Coming Home
37 in., 1992
Martin Freedman, Cabinet Maker

THE SACRED CIRCLE

The basic way we look at ourselves in our classes is as a group traveling together. We undertake this journey as a collective circle, rather than as individual makers, in order to mirror for each other the mystery of what lies within us. No one can see his or her own face alone; each person needs a mirror. And whatever we see in that mirror, for better or worse, must first be accepted before it can be transformed.

Let's imagine then you have this dream of re-creating something in yourself. You have sensed something stirring within you, something both disturbing and fascinating. It might manifest itself as anxiety or depression, but behind it you intuit an opening, an opportunity to create a new self. Now, inspired by the doll images and stories, you begin to believe that with the right attitude and within a supportive circle, this re-creation might occur. So you decide to accomplish what before seemed impossible. At least you decide to try.

You may never have made anything before. Or you may not be used to traveling with others. You may have lost faith in yourself, or grown weary and isolated in your life. And yet, to everyone's amazement, including your own, you have decided to pursue an obscure sacred art form. Unbelievably, you have committed to meeting for two-and-a-half hours each week for an entire year with the same group of strangers.

Looking around the studio you find that the group is quite varied: men and women of all ages, races, and professions. Everyone else, in your opinion, knows why they are there and seems much less fearful than you feel. No one appears that interested in what you do for a living, or how many children you have, or even what your name is. Instead, they want to know what do you really want from life? What is the ground you are standing on? What personal insight brought you here to make a doll? How do you wish to re-create the image of who you are? Sitting in this circle on a winter's day with fifteen strangers, you're now being asked to make a foot out of porcelain clay. You wonder, as you stick your hands into this amorphous piece of wet gushy earth: How in the world am I going to transform myself with this simple clay? Then, seeing that everyone around you is in the same boat—Charon's boat about to embark on a rite of passage—you squeeze the clay and begin.

Sanctuary
56 in., 1992
Cathy DeForest, Mother/Organizational Consultant

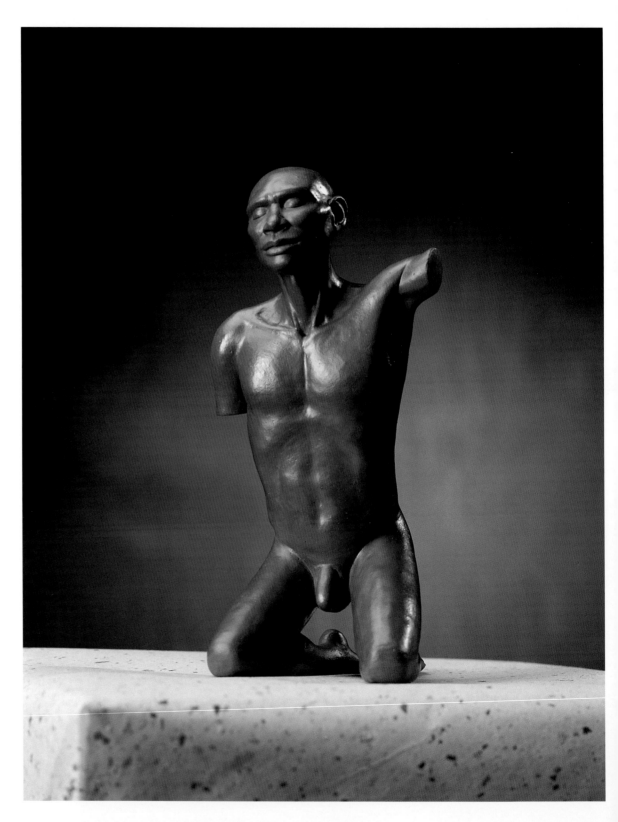

Dreamer
8.5 in., 1992
Joy Kelly, Dental Technician

"Oh, clay of the river, bend to our hands

Curve delicately.

See the strong shoulder and narrow neck.

Strip by strip and layer by layer,

Supple fingers kneading,

Long fingers molding,

Stiff thumbs shaping,

The beautiful pot, the pot of our mother."

—Didinga tribe (Uganda)

Girl Out of Water
33 in., 1990
Eliza Dudley Clark, Teacher/Artist

THE WAY OF CLAY

With porcelain clay we take in our hands a perfect mirror to reflect the work we are doing with our souls. By its nature, clay is an amorphous material. We all possess bodies and because we use them everyday, have attained a feeling-memory of the human form. Our hands have within them the capacity to translate this body-memory into clay. If we are not held back by negative feelings of doubt or unworthiness, we will find ourselves naturally forming representational images.

These images can guide us, like dreams do, to what else needs shaping. If we follow our feelings as they move through the clay, our instinctual creativity will guide us back to the most ancient of wisdoms: the wisdom of our interconnectedness with all things, all bodies, all matter, even humble clay. If, however, we find ourselves disconnected from this ancient wisdom, we usually discover in its stead the source of our original wounding. We all begin life in a primal relationship of wholeness. Between ourselves, others, and the world there is no disconnection. Unconsiously, we never forget this. It is the sundering of this primal wholeness—what we call "the original wounding"—and the instinct to repair that split, that throbs at the root of our creative urges. We have found, over the years, that when light is shed on this painful wound of separation, we usually discover an undeveloped and needful child, longing to return home.

From the first day in doll school we observe your fingers forming a foot in clay. Your doll, created from the most sincere intentions, is initated in those first tender, terrified moments. It is in that instance that we, as a compassionate circle, recognize and welcome the child within you.

The Guide and the Baby
54½ in., 1992
Jessica Elizabeth Kline, Developmental Therapist
for Brain Injured Children

Thus the clay, as the medium that reveals inner truth, reduces everyone and the work they do to child's play. At the same time, the circle provides love and supports the child within you. We might ask a dollmaker making a foot, "How does this foot reflect your present self? What is the ground that it now stands on?" If there is no image of wholeness reflected back then the clay work will mirror the inner conflict that is blocking the maker. At the center of this conflict there may sit a tyrannical critic dictating that nothing you do or say is right. This lack of self-love is usually expressed in many aspects of life. But here it is most concretely visible, to the dollmaker and to the circle, in the foot—the shape it takes, the force it embodies, the form it seeks to find. A dollmaker might realize then, while the rest of the circle witnesses and sympathizes, that it is not only a doll being crafted, but a soul. One may be shocked to find that their soul lived in a basement, hounded by negative feelings and attitudes. We teach that to change these attitudes you must consciously use the images and voices inside you. Demons and angels cohabit there, and if one listens when they speak, they will act as guides on this journey of re-creation. The spirit of this re-creation lives in the clay, in the process, and in the stories that, as the clay takes form, we tell and retell to each other.

Isabelle Come Home
68 in., 1993
Eva Helene Sax, Special Education Teacher/Speech
Pathologist

To the Known, Long Forgotten Place
Pieter/Peter, 32 in.; Mr. Kandle, 43 in.;
Helen/Helga/Katrin/Kate/Ann, 39 in.; Future, 41 in., 1993
Ingrid Lillemor Cole, Mother

Avalon
36 in., 1992
Pamela Davis, Designer/Writer

"Down a different path my knowing guide

leads me out of the still air into the trembling."

—Dante

Destiny
32 in., 1990
Cassandra Light

THE GUIDE

I have spoken so far about the doll and the doll process in terms of personal stories—in this case, of myself, the founding of the school, and the encouragement provided and nourished by a circle of students. But the nature of the process is to move beyond the personal; to align with larger patterns and seek out the greater archetype or myth in which one's personal story can be assimilated and transformed. In attempting this we need to look inward for something not as immediately tangible as personal histories, porcelain clay, or a circle of sympathetic people. We need to discover, through faith and imagination, our guide.

Every journey that moves from the world of dreams into that of wakefulness, that pushes what was unconscious into conciousness, is necessarily a guided one. The ancients understood this well. Aeneas was guided through the Underworld by Hecate; Dante through the Inferno and Purgatorio by Virgil. Ancient Greeks considered all intercourse between immortals and mortals to be mediated by messenger spirits or guides called *daimons* (of which the greatest was Eros). However you choose to think of your guide, however you envision him or her, the conviction that there is some guiding presence within you is absolutely necessary. If you do not have faith in your guide, the obstacles and confusions, the wrong turns and darkened corners of the journey, will leave you lost and baffled. So we implore one another throughout the process, whenever uncertainty arises, to conjure up our own guide: Who is he or she? What is your guide trying to tell you? What is the image he or she is holding or leading you toward?

I discovered my guide in the very first doll class. Over the past twenty years my guide has appeared to me in many forms, often as a young Asian woman. Though only a few people actually create their guide as a doll, I felt compelled to do so from the start. I've made this figure several times over the last decade. I am making her now. Presently she is Euphrosyne,

Hermes
30 in., 1992
Cassandra Light

a bird woman, one member of a group of Graces offering joy. She has also manifested herself as Persephone, Melancholia, and Autumn. What I know of her is expressed in my desire to bring her image and teaching into physical form. I think the symbolic character that best describes her is that of "muse." Her realm is the feminine, and the feeling she is most at home with is human grief. Charity is her name. She is related to the Greek Charities or Graces, dispensers of charm, beauty, and favor—as well as gratitude for these favors. She inspires the wisdom of music, poetry, and art. She speaks to me through the language of clay. As I work on her, I hear and intuitively see what to do next. I follow her direction. My students see the pain and delight I take in this experience. They see the faith I have in my guide and the results that faith produces. By watching me, and others who have given themselves over to being guided, my students begin to cultivate a belief that they too have a guide who will accompany them on their difficult journey.

Imagining one's guide then is a way of making a bridge between the unconscious and the conscious; between that which is hidden (one's original wounding) and that which becomes revealed (the finished doll and its story). If we open our eyes and ears we might begin to sense that there are guides all around us. They are in the dream that somehow brings an enlightening image; in the smell of lavender which evokes someone long forgotten; or in the inspired conversation struck up with an utter stranger. A guide might even be involved in how you came across this book.

If we ask sincerely for direction in the making of our doll, we will find our guide speaking to us through the clay figure forming in our hands, the piece of cloth and jewelry instinctively put together, or the cryptic, plaintive poem uttered out of nowhere. In all of this we are not calling upon supernatural forces, but merely seeking a form of messenger, a way to

Offering Grace
9 in., (Cabinet, 69 in.), 1993
Cassandra Light

communicate with the divine within ourselves. Such a path of connection is what, properly speaking, a metaphor is: a vehicle or other transport from one side to the other. In this sense, the entire doll process, from initial inspiration to the journey into darkness with a group of fellow travelers to the final emergence of a recreated self embodied in a doll, can be seen as a metaphor, a boat to bear us from one psychic state to another—a guide.

"O chestnut tree, great-rooted blossomer,

Are you the leaf, the blossom, or the bole?

O body swayed to music, O brightening glance,

How can we tell the dancer from the dance?"

—W. B. Yeats

Pit Fire Ritual, September, 1993
Photo by G. Frank

THE RITUAL

Although we consider this a spiritual process, religion or lack of religion, in our experience, doesn't effect the contribution any one individual makes. What matters is to practice expressing our connectedness to all living forms. Our chief way of doing this is through the observing of rituals. It is through these observations that the images, quotes, poems, and stories in this book came into being. They bear testimony to a powerful fact: that there is wisdom in everyone. And though individually expressed, this wisdom is collective.

The cycles of this wisdom, embodied in our rituals, are larger than mere human cycles. They include the cycles of creation, self-preservation, and destruction inherent in all life-forms. And for us, perhaps the most essential of these cycles is that of the yearly seasons.

We can identify our own creative process with the foliage we see out the window. Like the white-blossomed plum tree, we too are involved in an ongoing process of becoming. That's why, at those times when we begin to disbelieve our own creative process, when we get lost in too much analysis or judgment, we need only to look out at the tree. As long as it is cared for and nurtured, it will bear fruit. And so will we. The tree's creative story points to this truth through the language of natural objects. No matter how we imagine God, we best recognize our connection to all living things through the metaphors of nature.

Throughout the doll year we observe this language of nature within ourselves and in the outside world. The year begins for us at Hallowmas (late October), which is the time of the Doll Show and the time of All Souls. We honor, through the Doll Show itself, the spirits of all dolls, past and present, and also, by forming the classes for the next year, anticipate the dolls to come. At Winter Solstice we acknowledge the return of the sun by conducting group give-away ceremonies and plant the seeds of our intentions for the coming year—for

Amelia
58 in., 1993
Selma Aslin, Retail Business Owner

both ourselves and for our dolls—by speaking them to each other. There are further observances throughout the year, at Candlemas (February 2nd), Spring Equinox, Beltane (May 1st), Summer Solstice, and Lamas (August 2nd). These rituals change from year to year. One might have to do with making amulets or charms, another with telling stories from the past, writing poems, or offering fruit. Through these observances we link ourselves and our dolls to the materials from which we and they are created, to Nature and to the four seasons. In this way we remain conscious of what part we play in the larger story, of how our process of transformation is a microcosm of greater processes going on all around us. At Fall Equinox, we hold a final ceremony in which all the circles of that year, along with their families, come together at the beach and build a great bonfire and a giant earth mother made of sand. We make offerings and re-examine our original intentions. In this way we pay homage to the community we have become and, at the same time, recommit ourselves to the final challenge of bringing that year's Doll Show into being.

So the clay work, the storytelling, the sacred circle and the seasonal relationships we share with the sun and moon, the flora and fauna—all the strivings we undertake toward connectedness—are woven into a tapestry of rituals: a tapestry in which we are the weavers, the dolls are the figures, and the Doll Show itself the final design.

Persephone & Narcissus
45 in., 31 in., 1990-91
Claudia Albano, Public Relations Consultant

"When it comes—just so!

When it goes—just so!

Both coming and going occur each day.

The words I am speaking now—just so!"

—Musho Josho

Conscious Matter
60 in., 1992
Patricia Ellerd, Educator

THE DOLL SHOW

Most of the people featured in this book knew little or nothing about the school or our work before coming to a Doll Show. Many thought they were going to see a display of children's playthings. Very few were prepared for what they found. Many returned later, staying as long as three or four hours, looking at each doll, reading carefully its maker's story of transformation. Some were moved to tears by a doll. They often went home and told others to come see this extraordinary event. But just what is this Doll Show, that it creates such a stir in people?

The Doll Show seems to appear out of nowhere, like some magic theater or carnival, in a very large warehouse space. Within a week this empty space is transformed into a kind of mythic theater where more than a hundred dolls, some larger-than-life size, have been arranged in elaborate tableaux. Each will have next to it a poetic text, written in the dollmaker's hand. This text tells something of each dollmakers' journeys and how making the dolls led them to discover what they needed to find in themselves. This event, which lasts only two weeks, is witnessed by more than 5,000 people, almost all of whom hear about it by word of mouth.

The other important facet of the Doll Show is that it completes a cycle of discovery, creation, struggle, and fulfillment—and at the same time begins another. For it is by experiencing the Doll Show that people are inspired to embark on the next year's journey. So the journey, the process, the circle continues, born again and again out of its own completion. "The end," as T.S. Eliot forever reminds us, "is where we start from."

Road Warrior
36 in., 1992
Grant Davis, Physical Therapist

From the opposite direction, there are also people who come into the circle loud and incapable of listening. They learn through the doll work to quiet themselves, recognizing that there is a language of silence.

Whether we have a desire to speak or to be silent, we always strive to appreciate and give words to the true self that dwells within each of us.

She Who Knows
46 in., 1992
Susan Laing, Artist

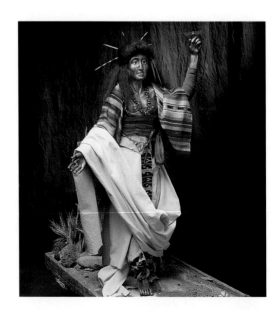

"It is possible that the scream that comes from the forsaken body, the scream that manifests in a symptom, is the cry of a soul that can find no other way to be heard. If we have lived behind a mask all our lives, sooner or later—if we are lucky—that mask will be smashed. Then we will have to look in our own mirror at our own reality. Perhaps we will be appalled. Perhaps we will look into the terrified eyes of our own tiny child, that child who has never known love and who now beseeches us to respond. This child is alone, forsaken before we left the womb, or at birth, or when we began to please our parents and learned to put on our best performance in order to be accepted. As life progresses, we may continue to abandon our child by pleasing others. That child who is our very soul cries out from underneath the rubble of our lives, often from the core of our worst complex, begging us to say, 'You are not alone. I love you.' "

—Marion Woodman

Breaking and Mending

The doll process, like the doll itself, is made of many parts. For the doll: porcelain feet, hands, and face; a metal and wood skeleton; bound cotton for muscle; raw silk for skin; glass eyes, a wig, a costume, and finally, a setting or tableau. For the process: initial intentions put into words; a circle of fellow travelers; the telling and retelling of stories; the encountering of clay; the reopening of a wound; the learning how to follow a guide; the rituals and seasonal observances and, finally, the Doll Show.

But in the end, as in the beginning, all of these parts make up a single story. And the story is always a human story; always different, always the same. So we conclude where we began—with a tale.

The Child-Artist Tale

There was a woman who, when she first came to the doll school, wanted to make something that would bring more pleasure into her life. Then, after working through the process she came to realize she wanted something more specific: She wanted to become an artist. Having spent most of her adult life as a physical therapist she, at age forty, found herself desiring a complete career change. She was quite gifted and perfectly capable of becoming a professional artist. As we listened to her story, however, we became aware of something blocking her desire. She spent a great deal of her creative energy overworking and keeping busy, as if there were something she was trying to avoid. At this point we attempted to locate the obstacle in her path by asking: What sort of doll could lead you to fulfilling your desire? For this woman it was a doll that would teach her how to open up to, and enjoy, a state of pleasure.

Black Horse Man Conjuring the Beloved
14 x 34 in., 1991
Sharon Hendrick, Physical Therapist/Artist

Motherspirit
18 in., 1992
Sharon Hendrick, Physical Therapist/Artist

As a young child this woman delighted in making pictures. Once, when she was very young, her parents laid her down on their bed for a nap. In a flurry of creativity, she scratched a design into her parents headboard with a bobby pin. When her parents returned and discovered her well-meaning but misplaced artistic efforts, they spanked her. In addition, they confiscated her crayons. As an adult, this woman felt blocked in her creative desires and felt this incident might have linked her creativity with a fear of punishment in her inner child's mind.

It is important to remember that these memories surfaced while this woman and the others in her circle were working on their dolls. This constant interaction between clay making, storytelling, and group ritual is what makes the doll process unique as a form of self-investigation. This woman already knew there was a relationship between her childhood and her adult ability to experience pleasure. But it was only when she got deeply into the clay work and found herself sculpting a small, carefully crafted figure that she began to relate the events of her childhood to her problems with creativity. She now revealed to us that at an early age, unbeknownst to her parents, she had been molested by an adult she trusted. She became quite distraught in speaking of this because, as she held her own small figure in her hands—that of a woman giving birth to herself—she suddenly recalled that the man who had molested her had also carved very beautiful figurines of nude women and children.

An inquiry into the small personal story that repeats itself can often expand our awareness of what is, for the individual soul, a larger mythic story. By listening to this woman's tale as well as observing her clay work and her doll's emergence, her larger story unfolded. She had first found innocent pleasure in art; but suddenly, as a result of the sexual abuse, she began to sense that there was something wrong with taking pleasure, especially in creativity. The

man who molested her was originally a good friend with whom she experienced delight and fun, and whose creativity she admired, but, again, creativity was linked with a shameful act. As these experiences came up in class, this woman became more and more aware of the complexes that were blocking her attempts to re-create herself. With this awareness she began to reshape, through her doll, her attitudes toward creativity and pleasure.

The doll this woman created was a meditation on sustaining pleasure. It was an alchemical healing doll, bare breasted with horns. With her doll, she was able to locate the pleasure in touching the clay and stayed in it. Her feet did not stop at the ankle, but extended up the leg. She shaped the face and then the neck and even began to sculpt the breasts. The doll that emerged from this woman's hands continually offered its teaching: "Taking pleasure in creating is good; go on, continue." It was at this point that this woman began to think seriously about becoming an artist. Then, as her piece neared completion, a traumatic but often necessary part of the process erupted: during the kiln firing, her doll's clay head split in two.

Suddenly, this woman was thrown back to her original wounding. Her relationship to something she had created out of love and desire was again under attack by the Fates.

But this time she was conscious of how this psychic pattern had entered her life. Even more importantly, she was not alone. Her loving circle witnessed this woman's grief. They all understood how much healing her doll had accomplished. They believed that her wholeness, as well as her doll's, could be restored. They told her how remarkable and unique she was. They offered their support and assistance unconditionally, containing for her, like some sacred vessel, the faith and courage she needed to mend the break between herself and her creative process.

Sherlin
55 in., 1990
Sharon Hendrick, Physical Therapist/Artist

The healing doll was successfully mended. The break was not irreparable and the message was not punitive but instead, inspirational: In every shattering, every cracking open, there is a new and unexpected chance to re-unite. And so, although some of the crack still shows in this woman's doll, it now serves as a very human reminder that behind every scar is a wound that has been healed.

This woman has gone on to become an artist. But what seems just as important to us is her story. It is a whole story now, embracing both innocence and wisdom, pleasure and pain. Without the breaking and the mending, the wounding and the healing, we would not know what her soul was capable of. When we create something without love, there is no loss when it is taken from us. Conversely, when we make a heartfelt commitment to something, then its loss compels us toward a new spiritual perspective that inspires us to see loss as an opportunity for change. We may be able to transfigure the break or mistake into an experience of wholeness.

The truth of being human is that we are mortal and with that truth we all live and die. We are all in a process of creating, preserving, and destroying our physical bodies. The impermanent physical nature of the doll, like our own bodies, is not of great importance to the larger story, but the love that these bodies generate is.

The spiritual perspective we strive for in our classes is only arrived at by giving ourselves over to love: to love for what we create, to love of beauty and liberation, and to love for humanity and all living things. These are for us the absolute spiritual mirrors.

At first I did not know what my doll was going to be until my dad died. I decided it was going to be an angel to help me. I am her best friend. She is my favorite angel. From the heavens she can look through her crystal ball and see everything and everybody on earth. Her job is to listen and understand people. I feel she really understands me.

The Realms

*"The archetypes are the imperishable elements
of the unconscious, but they change their shape
continually…the most we can do is dream
the myth outward and give it modern dress."*

—C. G. Jung

People make different types of dolls to explore different areas of their psyche. (The word *psyche* means "soul" in Ancient Greek.) We have used the word soul throughout this book and spoken of "soul making" as a way to describe the process of creating a doll.

If we think of the psyche as an actual place, as a form of geography, then we might begin to notice certain changes in the landscape. There are deserts, forests, islands, and mountains. While they all make up one planet, one psyche, soul, or world, they do slope off into various demarcations which we, in the context of the dolls, have chosen to call "realms." Over fifteen years and almost a thousand dolls, the realms that have emerged seem to fall into these categories: The Human, The Personality, The Feminine, The Masculine, and The Quintessence. When we pass from one realm to another, we move from one geography to another—from one area of the soul to another. The images you see here are organized around these realms. Think of them as the intention that generated both the doll and the story before you. Every doll came from one process and every doll came from a specific realm.

Each realm contains a brief definition as well as the personal story of a dollmaker, like the one you might read at the Doll Show. We've also included photographs of various dollmakers and their creations, along with other statements and evocations to create the gestalt for that realm.

It is our sincere wish that as you travel through the realms of this book you will be surprised and inspired by what ordinary people, when brought together in a supportive circle, can create out of their unconscious. We hope that it will encourage you to become a maker too. For as Diotima said to Socrates: "Every passage of non-being into being is poetry, or making. And the process of making any art is creative."

Mary Alice
72 in., 1992
Barbara Fess, Mother

THE HUMAN

The dolls that dwell in the human realm reflect their maker's experience of the mythic through typical human relationships: the loving or withholding mother; the protecting or tyrannical father; the wounded or innocent child; the wise or foolish elder, even the beloved pet. What sets these dolls apart from those of other realms is that they always represent someone from real life—a person not from legend, myth, or mask, but from history.

Often these dolls serve as memorials for a lost loved one, or as part of a scene reenacted to heal wounds inflicted by, or to, other human beings. Many lost or abandoned children have been brought into being, eternally reaching out for a parent who never comes. These images are almost always dressed in the common clothes of our lives. We recognize in them the stories we share about being human. If you discover in your personal story the recurrent demoralizing attitudes of an inner critic, you might turn to creating a grandfather or grandmother whose image offers you unconditional love. Or you might find yourself

My Mother, Anna
40 in., 1992
Ellen Rosenau

My Grandfather, Joe Forss
48 in., 1992
Jeanine Augst, Real Estate Broker/Librarian

The Blessed Child and Carmen Haynes
Photo by Margo Weinstein

Ted
72 in., 1991
Thaddea Pojanowska, Accountant

making a demonic father or mother and, by re-creating that terrible parent, begin to free yourself of an inner tyrant. Many shadowy human figures have been released this way into the world of form and light.

There usually resides, in these real-life images, some specific healing or message needed to further one's journey. Many have begun their clay work envisioning some archetypal being, only to have a figure from their past or present emerge, garbed in common threads, pointing to the realm of the human as their pathway to the mythic.

THERE WAS A STUDENT WHO, from a very early age, imagined that everywhere she went some terrible shadow was about to overtake her. Though there seemed, from outward appearances, nothing to be afraid of, she acted as if she was in a constant state of hiding. One day she casually asked her father where his parents were. Her father, who had never spoken of the Holocaust, reacted angrily to her innocent question by yelling, "Those Nazi

Fanny Meyer
48 in., 1990
Sacha Meyer-Kawaichi

bastards killed them!" Her father had, for the first time, given a name to her shadowy fears. Yet, neither "those Nazi bastards" nor her grandparents were ever spoken of again. The household seemed to contain some invisible nemesis, obscurely felt yet never mentioned. As she grew up, these unconscious fears played themselves out. By the time she was an adult she had developed a neurological disorder that caused her voice to trill as if overcome with emotion. When you first heard her speak there was no question she sounded upset, even though often she wasn't. It was as if her family's unexpressed feelings about the Holocaust were running rampant through her trembling voice.

When this student began making a doll, she thought she was creating a compassionate peasant woman. As the process went on, her needs and fears tumbled out, but without any discernible names or forms. She needed a recognizable container for her feelings, which the doll provided. Finally, near the end, as she began dressing the doll, its true identity was revealed. The doll was her paternal grandmother, killed in the Holocaust. This shadowy image, buried for so long in the unconscious, was finally released.

In the end, this woman not only heard her grandmother's voice inviting her to reclaim a lost existence, but also found a new self-confidence when expressing her feelings. She became more accepting of the trill in her voice—acknowledging it as an aspect of herself—as she gave form to the shadows inside her. This doll has been shown often over the years, and her story has moved many. Frequently, witnesses who see this lost Jewish grandmother allow themselves, perhaps for the first time, to openly grieve the tragic losses of the Holocaust.

Melanie
25 in., 1993
Monica Clark, Newspaper Editor

Monica Clark

On May 17, 1991, I became part of a national statistic—the one woman in nine diagnosed with breast cancer. In the weeks of surgery and radiation that followed, I embarked on a journey toward health that took me far beyond ridding my body of malignant cells.

Through the doll process, I traveled back forty-seven years to meet a frightened three-year-old who stood at the foot of a half-constructed stairwell, waiting for a loving hand to guide her into her new home. Instead she heard herself being chided for her fear of the unknown and harshly reproved for disrupting her parents' anxious tour of the house.

The setting of our meeting was clay, the moist mud of childhood revisited. It was not a happy encounter. The three-year-old at the foot of the stairs and the grown woman trying to sculpt a clay foot were both paralyzed by the fear of making a mistake. Inside me, parental voices resounded: "We love you when you get it right." My familiar defense—trying harder—didn't work. Finally I abandoned my struggle to fashion an adult-sized foot. My hands wanted to mold a child's foot. Her face emerged. It was me again, three years old, innocent, and frightened. Then her hands, disproportionately large, reached out.
She spoke:

> *I stand here alone,*
> *a somber little girl,*
> *yearning to be picked up,*
> *held,*
> *told that I too am wonderful.*

See into my aching soul,

my desire for a playmate,

my exhaustion at trying

to be good enough

to earn a place in someone's heart.

Who will love me?

Who will embrace me while

I learn to love myself?

The child and the grown woman wept. So many years of striving for perfection had created an emotional cancer that was destroying my soul as surely as the other cancer was afflicting my body. Through hesitant tears and with halting voice, I held out my need—I held out my doll.

One by one my classmates approached. They hugged my doll. They embraced me. Clay and community merged, and my confidence, wrenched apart so long ago, began to mend.

It was a transforming moment. But it was not a transformation. That is the challenge of a lifetime, faced one faltering step at a time. The Way of the Doll is no easy trip. It is a slow, labored, labyrinthine quest.

The miracle is that I've begun.

Gnome Crone Shamaness
and Heidi Lucas Page
Photo by Margo Weinstein

Bird Mother
16 in., 1992
Victoria Brost Aberg, Landscape Architect/Mother

THE FEMININE

The feminine realm is primarily concerned with bringing intuitive insight to physical and emotional conflicts. It arises from the dream and the dance of the instincts. It is the realm of inspiration, of the Sirens and Furies haunting our depths, of sibyls and crones conjuring mysteries. It is the sensual vessel, the womb where we're nourished, absorbed, destroyed, and preserved. Where the masculine pushes up into form, the feminine beckons us down into feeling, deeper even, into being.

The kind of doll, its age and station in life, indicate what lost aspect of the feminine the maker is trying to restore. So, making a baby girl usually has to do with a restoration of purity and innocence; creating a young girl or maiden with awakening inspiration and sexuality; making a mother figure with returning to a loving maternal connection; and fashioning the figure of an old woman or crone with embracing the nature of what life has,

Untitled
30 in., 1993
Jill Ross, Mother

Aral at the Stillpoint of the Turning World
64 in., 1993
Larissa Bruehn, Occupational Therapist

of her. The whole scene seemed to physically reveal what had been unconsciously going on in this woman, blocking her fertility. The dark, invisible force that held down her instinctual sexuality was released. By binding him herself, she had finally contained and redirected his destructive influence on her. The baby flew behind her, a lost hope, but one restored to consciousness and wholeness.

One month after the Doll Show—after completely letting go of her maternal desires—this woman joyfully announced to all of us that she was at last, to her total surprise, pregnant.

In June of 1994, she gave birth to a baby boy and called him Benjamin.

Geneen Roth

Rosebud
55 in., 1992
Geneen Roth, Author

I didn't intend this doll. I thought I was making a Native American man, an elder with white hair in a long ponytail and coal dark eyes. He came to me at the beginning and end of class, at home in my rocking chair. I thought these were his feet. And then the head began to take shape. When the lips and nose emerged, I knew immediately who she was. Rosebud.

As a child, I learned to put myself away, slip through a plane of silver light in my chest and make myself flat. Rosebud is everything I could not be, feel, know: She takes up space. She honors her appetites for food, solitude, love, beauty. She knows that if you abuse the body, you damage the soul.

Rosebud emerged from what I saved and from where I put myself when I "went away." She walked out whole and wild, fearless and self-contained. She knows that a girl-turning-woman is full with the moon, heavy as branches of apple blossoms in spring, and she is not afraid of her bounty. She allows her own lushness, lets her body be every ripening inch of itself because she is who she is and knows the possibilities to which she could give birth.

She stands now in my writing room. I look from my work, see the glint of a butterfly's wing, the feet pulling the earth up, up into her legs, hands, womb. And in moments of fear and despair, when I have forgotten who I am, she whispers to me: Everything lost can be found again.

Everything lost can be found again.

Kagingakah-Green Man
61 in., 1991
Grant Davis, Physical Therapist

Warrior King
65 in., 1992
Janet Wilson

THE MASCULINE

Dolls made from the masculine realm are usually created out of a dollmaker's desire to reclaim some necessary strength or courage in their outer life. It is a realm of power, knowledge and order; of structured boundaries and systems; of cadenced time and measured space. It is filled with heroes, princes, and kings of justice; with tyrants, ogres, and giants of inscrutable force. On the human scale, it may emerge as an internalized father figure, idealized or demonized. This masculine archetype almost always appears in some area where consciousness is needed. He comes to announce a change or growth in awareness. If the figure is a warrior, he might indicate a struggle for courage and foresight. A green man or vegetative god might auger a coming dismemberment and regeneration. A prince or young native boy might suggest the emergence of some new skill or capacity; an old wise man, the acceptance of age, or the experience of totality. Making the king can express a need for structure, or a desire for security and protection. The erotic masculine, who we call Eros, is the power that drives this realm, translating the scattered into the ordered, the mute into the articulated, the mundane into the divine. He is the dynamic god within us that penetrates the formless unconscious, thrusting into our everyday awareness a dominant and transforming image.

THERE WAS A STUDENT WHO was adopted by a wealthy couple when she was an infant. The couple wanted a child to complete their family and build their future. This child became their "golden girl," always striving to achieve the goals and tasks she believed were the requirements of success in her family. This family was dominated by her grandfather, a powerful, larger-than-life public figure who exerted his will over the others. It was a realm of very conditional acceptance, one that included, above all else, the keeping up of appearances—even to the point of cosmetic surgery.

Zukaro and Gino Valente
Photo by Margo Weinstein

Hanged Man
72 in., 1992
Diane Smith, Feldenkrais Practitioner

When this woman came to the doll class, she began to make a very large figure of a man. His largeness became a kind of class joke, but inside this joke was an intimate truth necessary to this woman's survival: she needed, had always needed, someone huge and dominating to protect her, to champion her right to belong in her adopted family. She had, since early adulthood, dated only athletic, heroic-sized men between 6'4" and 6'8". This practice, she learned, was merely an attempt to find in the outside world what she needed to discover and affirm within herself. She was looking for someone accepting and gentle enough to love her for herself, yet big and powerful enough to fend off anyone—like her grandfather—who might try to dominate her. Her need manifested as an over-sized doll: her Warrior King. As the doll progressed she surrendered to his sovereignty and dressed him in clothes befitting a king. When he was finally placed in the Doll Show, his formidable presence provided a sacred dominion in which she could finally grow up. In her doll she had created the masculine protector she needed for the re-creation of herself.

The Protector of Murmur
64 in., 1993
Tony Karasch, Artist/Printer

The Boy Who is Listening for His Name
21 in., 1990
Kim Tozer McLaughlin,
Psychotherapist/Mother/Gardner

The Messiah Warrior
69 in., 1993
Steven Stern, Entrepreneur

The Merman
60 in., 1993
Audrey Von Hawley, Networker/Artist

Saigo
35 in., 1988
Donna Nomura Dobkin, Bookkeeper

Blessing Father
60 in., 1993
David Sheppard Surrenda, Organizational Psychologist

David Sheppard Surrenda

In kindergarten, I was given a white piece of paper and told to draw a picture. I didn't know how to do it. I remember it scared me more than anything I could imagine. When I finally did manage to draw something, it immediately became the object of my own ridicule. It was never as good as the other kids' drawings. I was always seeking right answers, and drawing had no "right" answers. I have, ever since, been terrified of the blank page. I associated drawing—all making of things out of nothing—with art; and I did all I could to distance myself from "being an artist."

It's not surprising then, that to sculpt a figure, amid a community of others, evoked my worst nightmares. Yet I was absolutely committed, because of where I was in my life, to proceed unflinchingly and face the uncertainty, judgments, and confusions that awaited me in this adventure.

My first job was to rid myself of anxiety about the outcome. I tried to approach each step without any specific sense of its expected result. Of how much value, after all, were my internal maps and guideposts in a territory I knew so little about?

My second job was to eliminate my need to be special. I was determined to be just an ordinary student with no great final product to strive for, or particular position to establish in some imaginary class pecking order. I was just going to be quiet, listen, and surrender to the flow of an uncertain process.

The third step was to give up my self-judgments. I felt helpless with my hands: they seemed too big, too clumsy, too imprecise. My eyes couldn't focus on small objects or make the discriminations necessary to thread a needle. But slowly, as I relaxed and gave over to the process, the unformed clay began to move within my fingers and take on recognizable form before my eyes. It actually *looked* like a foot. But ironically, this created another problem.

68

For it was just there that I would freeze, be afraid to go on, or to change whatever I'd made, in case it might lose its general familiarity of being a foot.

This was the final step I had to overcome. At a certain point I lost confidence in my ability to finish the object, to take it to the next level of beauty and aliveness. I decided to stop and accept that it wouldn't get any better. But my instructors gently urged me on. My fellow students were supportive. And miraculously it happened: with a little push here and there—coming from I don't know where—my foot suddenly looked more real, more alive and vibrant.

Finally, about eight months into the process, while creating my first ear (the most difficult part of the head to sculpt), time, space, judgment, and my past disappeared. I was finally "just there" with the clay and the quiet sensation of shaping an ear. It didn't really matter if it looked like an ear. I felt myself one with the work in a way that was present and fearless, fully engaged on every level with the human ear. From that moment on, my process was entirely different. It became an echo of laughter, the internal smile of someone who would not be stopped by history or fear. I was going to create simply for myself. I felt full and joyous in the work, no longer empty or haunted.

Today I go on, a perennial student, each year testing my new-found wings on some "inability" that in the past I would never have confronted. Someday, perhaps at the end of my life, I may laughingly say, "I really am an artist."

Peace
48 in., 1992
Alice Rubenstein, Physical Therapist/Feldenkrais
Practitioner

Rage
36 in., 1992
Alice Rubenstein, Physical Therapist/Feldenkrais
Practitioner

Little Frannie and Kethlenda the Banshee
61 in., 1991
Frannie Minervini Zick, Early Childhood Educator

The Believer
24 in., 1992
Joan Carlson, Graphic Artist

Untitled
36 in., (64 in.), 1992
Suzanne Hirshen, Community Organizer

THERE WAS A STUDENT WHO lived his life for his mother. As a child she protected and dominated him. If he tried to get his own way, her withdrawal of love was so painful that he chose to disown his life rather than be forced to live without love. By the time this son grew up, his only reason for being successful in the world was to please the women he loved. If a relationship ended, he felt compelled to deny the rest of his life: he'd move away, leave his job, friends and every other thing that was important to him. After many similar relationships and break-ups, he had sacrificed a successful career, lost his house, car, expensive clothes, and, most importantly, his attractive male persona.

One day a woman friend dragged this man to a Doll Show. He was so moved by the possibility of true acceptance he found there that he joined a doll class. As he began his exploration he found, amid the rubble of his past, an aging, broken man trying to recover his basic identity. He began to shape, in clay, a large, life-size figure of a lonely old man. It was his own worst fear, mirroring back to him his persona ten years from now: a doll sitting at a table in a small tenement, listening to pathetic love songs, and reflecting on lost loves

Rima
60 in., 1992
Corrinne Allison Farner, Somatic Practitioner

Moment
72 in., 1991
Natalie Robb, Artist/Teacher

Joy
48 in., 1992
Merrilee Levis, Acupuncturist/Herbalist

pictured in photos scattered across the floor. It was the shadow side of his lover identity—an almost cartoon version of himself, living in a place of passive suicide, resigned to never experiencing love's passions again. The framed room he made to display his doll had no actual walls, and anyone could enter without asking. There his doll sat in its self-made theater, embodying a desperate man with no boundaries or self-respect.

The reality of this vision was shattering to this man. For the first time he understood how his life had become a doormat for unrequited love. Once he saw the truth in what he had created, he consciously changed the tableau. He put up walls, asked people to enter only after knocking, got rid of the love songs and photos, and replaced them with a typewriter (so that he might write about his own life). The man sitting there in the end was still materially poor, but he was no longer spiritually impoverished. He was his own person living his life for himself for the first time.

Untitled
60 in., 1993
Barry Pullman, Drummer/Writer/Cook

Tragic Rat
71 in., 1992
Andy Smith, Interactive Television Producer

Andy Smith

When I was two years old, I was hospitalized for a contagious illness and brutalized very badly by well-meaning but unenlightened doctors. For two weeks that I can now barely remember, I screamed in a white, stainless-steel torture chamber. I was stabbed, cut, taped, and bound in isolation. I was so frightened that eventually I could only scream silently. I tried to escape every night and hurt my feet kicking, running, and falling in the linoleum darkness. Unable to flee from the real building, I learned that my only escape hatch out of that hell was through a secret passageway at the top of my head. Up and out was freedom; inside was only pain and terror. Today there is even a name for my experience: Medical Abuse Syndrome.

After I was released I began to develop an interest in machines—particularly airplanes. Eventually I decided that I wanted to become a scientist.

Twenty years later, I joined a biotechnology company as a lab technician. I was assigned to maintain the "Biological Testing Facility"—the room where the drugs were tested on animals. Like millions of other people trapped in life-negating jobs, I rationalized the underlying brutality of my work by thinking that it was for a greater good: healing the sick. The fact that it was the most promising job I'd ever had career-wise also kept me at it. Drinking took care of the rest of my discomfort.

The company was, I discovered after a few years, cynically run as a get-rich-quick scheme. Misleading press releases about imminent breakthroughs were put out to pump up the value of the stock with which all the top executives and scientists were being paid. At the bottom of the deception, in a sealed room with no windows that few dared to ever enter, was me; stupidly and naively following orders, five days a week, routinely committing unspeakable acts of cruelty against a multitude of trusting and frightened God-given spirits.

I am so sorry what I did to you, my beautiful and delicate friends. If I had not been so totally disconnected from my own pain-ridden paws, I never would have hurt yours so. Now I have indelibly added to my sense-memory the burden of your wounds. If such a thing is possible, through this doll, I ask the universe for forgiveness. I promise that your lives will not have gone in vain, and swear to devote my life to creating a world where no one must suffer as you did.

Tragic Rat (detail)

Old Woman, Dream Catcher, Demon, Listener, Seeker
and Lillian Lehman
Photo by Margo Weinstein

Old Woman
32 in., 1992
Lillian Lehman, Florist

Spirit of Planetree
40 in., 1990
Angie Theriot, Healthcare Reform Worker

THE QUINTESSENCE

The dolls pictured in this realm express, in subject and feeling, the essence of a quality: patience, faith, perseverance, joy. It doesn't really matter what particular sex, age, or culture they are. They represent a spiritual or poetic intention. Likewise, their stories, unlike the dolls in other realms, are not as necessary to their meaning. The dollmaker is trying instead to reveal a particular quality of being which he or she wants to integrate into themselves.

Like gold embedded in ore, the quintessence must be purified from its raw form. This alchemy of freeing the spirit from matter begins with the maker, contemplating the nature of his or her own dissatisfaction. By looking honestly into this mirror it is possible to find one's essential quality reflected back. For example, let's say that every time you try something new you are overwhelmed with fear. As a result, your clay will be shaped by that fear and hold it before you. You will then see that fear's opposite, trust, is needed, if you want to create this quality in your doll. In the same way, a person choosing to make a figure of devotion and love will have to explore in his or her own self-betrayal and hate. The opposite quality is always necessary to complement the alchemy of who you are trying to become. It is out of the act of unifying these opposites that the quintessence arises.

Phoenix and Adina
60 in., 40 in., 1993
Joan Tanzer, Social Worker
Photo by G. Frank

"When we journey to 'the other end of the world' to give substance to our psychic life, what awaits us is not Eden but all the contradictions of earthly life. We enlarge our capacity for understanding so that the world becomes transparent. Thus wise men retreat into solitude toward the end of their lives. But there is no sense in retiring before undertaking the journey. We meet love on the way, and whether it endures or dies, it makes life meaningful."

—Aldo Carotenudo

Doll Making, 1993
Photo by G. Frank

5

Way of the Doll

I have had over the years many great teachers. They have also been my students. Without their devotion and creativity, all this would not have been possible. There have been those among us who have risen from their common place at the table and acted, in the final days before the Doll Show, with great heroism, selflessly helping those around them. There have also been students whose painful teaching stretched me beyond my understanding. Every year brings both. Finally, after fifteen years imparting this work, I have come to grasp the nature of a truth which I feel T. S. Eliot best expressed: "The only wisdom we can hope to acquire is the wisdom of humility: humility is endless."

The practice of this humility is to admit one's failures as well as one's successes. Being a teacher, like being a parent, is a difficult and arduous responsibility. It bestows innocent love while demanding a conscious commitment to serve. I have not always risen to this calling, but I believe I have offered my sincere efforts toward its ideal. There have been those who have traveled with us, whose dark lessons of betrayal caused many souls to traverse an uncharted underworld. In these dark lessons we began to dream. To dream is a wonderful thing. To love, and then to leave that love in order to discover it in another form is one of the most painful and exacting journeys a soul can make. Did we ever think the way was clear? That it could be planned by anything other than our desire for wholeness? Do we know a language that can describe our unspeakable desire for fulfillment—a language that is human? For our attempts are always human attempts, vulnerable and poetic. It is a sad reaching out. But isn't it because of sadness that we find love and a reason to keep reaching?

Over the years there have been a few who return to the doll school for a second, third, or fourth year. Some have become artists or teachers of the process themselves. There was a man who came to me six years ago. He was the twenty-four-year-old boyfriend of a young

Wounded Chicken
38 in., 1991
Sammael Gromowsky, Multimedia Artist/Teacher

Happy Boy
20 in., 1993
Sammael Gromowsky, Multimedia Artist/Teacher

student of mine. When I met him he was working as an apprentice with a puppeteer at a local children's amusement park. He lived by himself, a reclusive, alienated artist on a horse ranch in the Oakland hills. I don't know why I asked him into a doll circle, but the sweetness of his face and smile immediately befriended me. We spoke after his first class, and the words that tumbled from his mouth were quite confused. His ideas about art and people, to any normal person, would have sounded paranoid and bizarre—a bit like nonsense. What I heard, however, was a truly creative visionary who had never been given responsibility, respect, or creative freedom. A short time after he entered the doll circle, one of the other

Childhood Into Adolescence
36 in., 1992
Sammael Gromowsky, Multimedia Artist/Teacher

Mother in Mind
12 in., 1991
Sammael Gromowsky, Multimedia Artist/Teacher

students, a psychologist, remarked to me that she was afraid he was psychotic. I did not believe this, and my instinct was correct. In a very short time he began to construct the skeletons for all the dolls; each week inventing, reorganizing, and re-creating new structures. In less than three months he became the creative engineer of the entire school. With his vision the Doll Show grew in size and scope. It became more theatrical, dramatic, and monumental. Nothing seemed impossible for this young man's imagination. If someone wanted their doll to walk, leap, or spin, he could spark it into action. After a time, the student who had misjudged him earlier commented on how unbelievably transformed he

Psyche's Sisters
36 in., 1993
Cassandra Light

will cultivate our fresh view. If we are older, we need to give generously of our resources and experiences to nurture that which will follow and restore us.

In our end is our beginning. To re-create a new life we need the warmth and security of the cocoon we weave together. But there comes a time when the chrysalis—its transformation into a butterfly completed—must break free and fly away. We have to loosen our woven circle of love, to separate as individuals, and follow wherever our soul's journey takes us. There is a sweet poignancy in the leaving. We began as strangers and are now fellow travelers standing proudly with our doll-guides. Now, as the year closes, the depths to which we

Time Master
20 in., 1993
Cassandra Light

committed ourselves to each other is felt in the final acknowledgments. In the last days of the Doll Show, we sit together in our individual circles and honor each person for what they contributed to our collective journey. We sum ourselves up, giving blessings and receiving them: We practice the language of fulfillment.

Forlorn
4 in., 1991
Cassandra Light

Jizo
30 in., 1991
Cassandra Light

Where do last year's travelers go from here? Some go on to other creative pursuits: writing, singing, acting; activities they never thought they could do, but now feel confident in committing to. Some continue making dolls or other forms of visual art. Still others continue to search for a spiritual, creative community. Others get married, have children, get divorced, buy houses, make career changes, knowing that wherever life takes them their newly awakened creativity need no longer be held back.

Often people ask me, what happens to the dolls? Many go to their makers' homes and hold an honored place in that person's life. A few, after a time, are ritually destroyed by their makers. These are usually people who need to bring closure to the experience the doll brought forth, or whose wounding was not fully worked out within the doll itself (shadow dolls often meet this fate). Years after they have made their dolls, I might get a letter or meet students on the street and they will speak to me of some creative activity they are pursuing. Most tell me that more than anything they still hear in themselves, like a mantra, something that was repeated in their circles, in their minds and hearts every week throughout the year in our meditations—an echo of support, an attitude of belief that has made their continuing re-creation possible:

> *"You are who you are and that is all.*
> *And that is all that needs to be."*
>
> —Cassandra Light

For some it is a lifetime struggle to learn this simple teaching. Others need unconditional love and support. Sometimes a guide must come forth and point out the path. But for us, in the Way of the Doll class, it takes all of these tasks and offerings, and still something more. It takes a doll.

Generations of Truth
Middi Kori Koti, 34 in.; Mamasi, 48 in.; Amajoli, 46 in.;
Baby Emi Dada, 20 in., 1993
Midge Robinson, Teacher/Artist/Spiritual Counselor

Afterword

After reading this book you might ask: How could I make such a journey? Who should I seek as a guide? I would respond: Whichever way is right for you, is right for you. I have been fortunate enough to have found my way. And I offer it here as one small example of what can happen when that way is found. It is my intention, not my expectation, that you too might find your way, your own teaching, and discover a language, a form, whatever it might be, that answers to that unique voice pulsing within you.

There was a student once who called me from Indiana. She had found my name in a book written by someone else. She had experienced a vision that healing could come from dolls. She was in search of others who might have had the same vision. She spoke to me of her aspirations to be a teacher. I encouraged her. I said, "Just begin." She asked me a question, which I lingered over for a long time: "Since not everyone who wants to take a doll class is able to, might I someday write a book?" She desired a book that would transmit what it could about the process, that might inspire her and others like her to open their channels and let their unique voices be heard. I shared her vision, but doubted my abilities as a writer. I told her that I hoped someday to have the courage to write such a book. For there are so many of us out there looking for each other. I was one lucky enough to be seen, heard, and believed. Now today, thanks to my students and colleagues; to all the writers and poets who have inspired me; and especially to my guide, Charity, this book has been written. As with the first doll class fifteen years ago, I have no idea where it will eventually lead. But to have made an effort, with sincere love and faith, is and will always be something worth doing.